ALSO BY ZACHARY MASON

Void Star
The Lost Books of the Odyssey

METAMORPHICA

METAMORPHICA

ZACHARY MASON

FARRAR, STRAUS AND GIROUX

NEW YORK

Farrar, Straus and Giroux
175 Varick Street, New York 10014

Copyright © 2018 by Zachary Mason
Printed in the United States of America
First edition, 2018

Maps by Bronwen Abbatista

Library of Congress Cataloging-in-Publication Data
Names: Mason, Zachary, 1974– author.
Title: Metamorphica / Zachary Mason.
Description: First edition. | New York : Farrar, Straus and Giroux,
    2018. | Includes bibliographical references.
Identifiers: LCCN 2017052979 | ISBN 9780374208646 (hardcover)
Subjects: LCSH: Ovid, 43 B.C.–17 A.D. or 18 A.D.—Adaptations.
Classification: LCC PS3613.A8185 M483 2018 | DDC 813/.6—dc23
LC record available at https://lccn.loc.gov/2017052979

Designed by Jonathan D. Lippincott

Our books may be purchased in bulk for promotional,
educational, or business use. Please contact your local bookseller
or the Macmillan Corporate and Premium Sales Department
at 1-800-221-7945, extension 5442, or by e-mail at
MacmillanSpecialMarkets@macmillan.com.

www.fsgbooks.com
www.twitter.com/fsgbooks • www.facebook.com/fsgbooks

1 3 5 7 9 10 8 6 4 2

For Keta Muessa Sumi-e Mason

Everything changes,
Nothing ends

—Ovid, *Metamorphoses*

CONTENTS

PART VII: DEATH

PART VIII: APHRODITE, CONTINUED

PREFACE

Myth should be essential, but often seems schematic, less a literature of fundamental power than that literature's echo. The project of *Metamorphica* is to write the mythology I wish I'd found, much as Ovid did, moving lightly through the ancient sources, taking up what he liked and reinventing it, as I've done with his book.

NOTE ON THE
STAR MAP

The brightest stars are stories.

The night sky is divided between Aphrodite, Athena, Zeus, Nemesis, Dionysos, Apollo and Death.

Stories appear in the septant of the most salient god, or on the boundary of the two most salient.

Lines are narrative connections which form constellations.

A story's distance from the center increases with its distance from primordial time. The outermost ring is the end of the age of myth, which is the aftermath of the Trojan War or shortly thereafter.

PART I

APHRODITE

1

OVID

Ovid was a Roman poet. An early success, he despised his own work. He sought out Aphrodite, Rome's tutelary goddess, in the hope of striking a bargain. He ended up exiled to the shore of the Black Sea.

Ovid walks at twilight through dry rolling hills. A woman is before him, trailing her hands through the tall grasses which smoke wherever her languid touch falls, blackening and writhing and turning to ash. Fire roars and pops behind them, ruddy serpents of flame seething over the hills, but she's singing a tuneless song and seems not to notice.

He's about to speak when she says, "Not literature for you, but the literary life, because you're lazy, and love company, and what you'd most like is to be famous without writing a word. Your work will be forgotten when you die, or a little before, though the memory of your persona will last a little longer."

"I know," he says. "That's why I found you."

"It would take exile," she says, still not looking back. "You'd have to give up everything. You would be transformed." He feels her waver for a moment, but then she says, "You wouldn't be willing."

"But I am," he says. "I'd give anything, everything . . ."

But she's lost interest, is already far ahead and getting farther, and his chance is gone, but he rallies against the inexorable momentum of events, chases after her and seizes her arm.

She turns on him like a serpent and he staggers back as the hand that touched her burns like dry wood, the fire pulsing up his arm, the black bones showing through his incandescing flesh . . .

GALATEAS

The sculptor Pygmalion carved a woman named Galatea out of marble and fell in love with her. Aphrodite brought the statue to life.

The island's high wild hills were strewn with worn marble boulders, one of which glowed for him with more than ordinary light. Running his hands over the worn, lichen-stained surface, he could feel her within, her form latent, waiting to reveal itself. The smooth marble was like skin, or what skin ought to be.

His slaves rolled the boulder into his workshop as he laid out his chisels, then left him, as he needed to be alone for his great work. He uncovered her eye first, and wished he hadn't, as it was difficult to work with her watching. He didn't know what her face would be as he cut away the marble but when he saw it knew it couldn't have been another. Day and night passed unnoticed; if he closed his eyes he could feel a pulse in the marble's veins, a hint of warm breath on his hand as he caressed her cheek. With only her feet still entombed, he felt a building excitement, as though he were on the verge of some great thing, a final revelation in stone.

He fell asleep on an afternoon of thunderstorms and intolerable pressure in the air and dreamed that Aphrodite appeared to him among foam and flame and torn flowers and as she turned away she said, *Desire is always imminent*. He woke then, and his sculpture was gone, just flakes of the stone on the floor and wet footprints leading out into the garden, and though he cursed and wept, scarred the floor with scattered tools, in his heart he was relieved, for he now saw she was flawed, had been from the beginning, and in the high wild hills there were other prisms of marble scattered among the ridges and valleys and in one was what he wanted.

3

POLYPHEMUS

Polyphemus the Cyclops was Poseidon's son. He abandoned the courts of Olympus. Odysseus later blinded him.

I found an empty island. I'd been wandering for years, after the war, letting ocean wash the blood away.

I made a garden of the island. I excavated pools in the shade, carved the ridges to make the wind sing, planted orchards in the valleys and shaped every branch. My tread wore roads in the hills over the centuries. Who I'd been slipped slowly away, and I felt I was becoming the spirit of the place, subsumed in its life and geology.

Sea-nymphs came in on the waves, and men, born on the wind in white-sailed ships. They marveled at being the first to find this paradise. They settled the lowlands, and I let them, though they cut down trees and scarred the earth with their ploughs and their laughter and woodsmoke drifted up to my eyrie. I

could have shattered their towers and houses and
driven them into the sea, but I'd had my fill of death
and killing, and nymphs and men are short-lived, as
are cities, so I waited.

During the days I kept to the heights, arranging the
stones and resculpting the mountains, but in the evenings a restlessness sent me walking in the lowlands
to watch the fires kindling in the farmstead windows.

One day at dusk I saw a shadow picking its way
over the hills. It stopped, hesitated, then approached
me, and I saw it was a woman. Men rarely saw me even
when they walked right by so I didn't move, and was
amazed when she looked up into my face and said,
"They say there's a giant who haunts the hills, but I
never believed it."

I said nothing, but she reached out and touched my
hand. I hadn't spoken in years, but I found my voice
and said, "Go home."

"What's your name?" she said. "Do you have a
home? Are you all alone here?"

I could have left and let her wonder if she'd dreamed
me, but the night was settling, and the lights were
glowing in the houses, and the dark closing in, and
I found myself starting to talk. I told her how I'd shaped
the island and its beauty. I told her of my long journey
through the seas, of the war that came before it, of the
cataclysms, the shattering violence, the fallen giants
mistaken for mountains, of my family and their enemies and their overweening pride. I went on for hours,
and only when the moon was rising did she put her

hand on my knee and say her name was Galatea, and she'd see me again. I sat there alone, remembering her hand's pressure.

I waited for her every night. I talked as though ridding myself of all the words accumulated over the years. She spoke rarely, but I thought she saw in me a way to escape the limits of her life.

I knew not to look in still water or mirrors, but found a pool and stared at my face. Deep wit, indomitable strength, the scion of a great house—in the balance they're as nothing beside ugliness. Happy are the young, the careless, the lovely.

One night when it was late she put her head on my lap, which I tried to ignore. I spoke at random, then kissed her. Fragrant hair, pliant mouth, the sudden knowledge of the taste of her. She tried to pull away but I held her close. She thrashed like a fish, her tunic tore and then I was left holding a piece of cloth as she ran down the hill into the dark. "Galatea!" I bellowed, and in the valley below the farmers' dogs started barking.

She didn't come back the next evening or the next. I tried to tend to my forests and my mountains but my mind would wander. All this over such a small matter, I thought. She'll be old in decades, dust in a century. Go through the motions of work, I told myself, and soon you'll be working in earnest.

I walked the ridgelines when the sun rose, scanning the fields and the beaches. Every day I walked the same route, and every day I didn't see her. Where my sight-lines were occluded I tore out trees and knocked down escarpments so all the island was visible but still I saw nothing.

One day in the hills I found Tiresias the seer, blindly watching the flight of passing gulls. When I approached he cried, "Nobody* will be your undoing!"

"I ask no more," I lied.

He said, "Nobody will mock your agony!"

"In fact, Galatea hasn't been kind."

"Galatea?" he said. "Today is the day you forget her."

I said, "Wine speaks louder than the god today."

He said, "It will happen in the cove with the rip, which you passed an hour ago, so they don't expect you to return," and then he walked away mumbling to himself, following the wheeling flocks of birds.

I went back to the cove, and the seer was right; there was Galatea, entwined with her lover in the sunlight on the hot sand. They were utterly absorbed in each other. I should've slipped away and vanished but my pride, which I'd thought I'd mastered, rose up and I thundered her name.

Her lover sprang to his feet. He was brave, poor fool, fumbling in his clothes for his sword, but I crossed the beach in two strides and swatted him into the cliff where his head left a corona of bright crimson on the sandstone.

She knelt by his body, her voice ragged as she called

*Nobody was Odysseus' *nom de guerre*.

his name—Acis—though his skull was shattered into fragments like a mosaic. Then she was upon me, battering my abdomen with her little fists; I disgusted her and always had—I was loathsome, unlovable, contemptible and weak, and the rest was lost in sobbing.

It was the first time I'd seen her naked. She wasn't the flawless eidolon I'd imagined, with her quaking flesh, tangled hair, running nose and misery. My gaze settled on Acis, who looked surprised. I closed my eye but still saw his blood glistening on the pale rock. "Listen to me," she said.

I fled. I went up to the ridgeline but she pursued me, picking her way up the slope, so I put more hills between us. I came to a beach and still I heard her calling me so I walked into the water, breasting through the waves. The seas are shallow there, and though I'd thought I'd stay forever I left my island behind.

I waded through the ocean for days. I had dolphins for company, and distant ships, and storm-clouds, and, always, Acis' face.

Eventually I found another island, remote and barren, less lovely than the first and not good for much but goats and solitude. I carved Acis' image into granite cliffs over the beach and made a shrine to him.

The island's people started coming to the shrine, offering jam and the first fruits of summer in hopes of a good harvest, many children, success in raiding. I go to the shrine at night to see how his image has weathered and to pray that his ghost will forgive me and his memory fade.

PART II

ATHENA

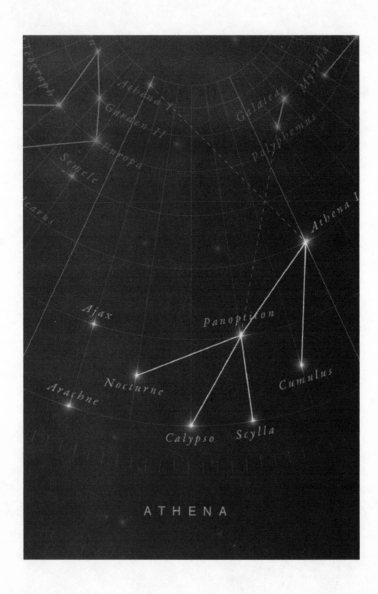

ATHENA

4

ATHENA II

Athena was the protector of heroes. She was partial to the intelligent. Odysseus, king of Ithaka, was her protégé.

He was always in my eyes. I stayed near him through the war, as a gull over the waves, a soldier in the line, a heat mirage on white sand. I turned arrows, spooked horses, crumbled his enemies' vertebrae in my hand. Nestor saw me, and might have known me, but, wise with years, said nothing.

There was a night when all the other Greeks were asleep in their tents and we two sat alone by the remnants of a beach-fire. The smoke obliged me to sit close to him. I was a young Cretan captain that night, someone he barely knew. He rarely mentioned Ithaka, but that night he spoke tenderly and at length of home and his Penelope. I didn't mind, for our bond was of another order.

"And what about you?" he said. "Is there someone waiting at home?"

"There is someone," I said.

"Wife?"

"No."

"Ah. Boy?"

"Yes."

"Peer or protégé?"

"Both," I said, and regretted it when he looked up at me and I saw that he was thinking.

"Someone younger than you, in need of your help, but his virtue such that, if it weren't for an accident of birth, you would be equals—yes?"

"Your understanding is deep," I said.

"Is he the kind to talk in riddles, or love someone who would?"

I became very still.

He poked the embers with a stick. Gulls floated in the moon-glow over the surf. "In such affairs," he said, "there are no dynastic issues, so it doesn't matter whether he was born prince or villein. My boy, I have no dog in any Cretan hunt, and there's no reason for you to hide anything from me. They say I'm insightful, so, come, tell an old man your trouble."

"I have to go now," I said, and vanished into the dark.

Troy would have fallen within a year, if I'd let it, but a stone, a fog, an order unheard can make nothing of near-victory, and Odysseus remained with me on the long beach between the looming battlements and the sea. I'd never been so happy.

·

I was sitting in the dunes one night when the sand was stained with white light and there was Aphrodite, floating before me, naked, her skin as pale and radiant as the moon. One hand hid her sex and the other her breasts and her head was turned away in what I thought was modesty but I saw her lips part slightly, saw that one hand crushed a nipple, that the other was moving. The end of my cut seemed to come at the same moment I drew my sword, but as I'd hit only air I turned and cut again, the blade biting deep into the sand. I looked around, sweating, but the span of beach was dark, silent, deserted.

Troy tottered; its heroes died, its allies slipped away in the small hours and its strong rooms stood empty. The Greeks could feel that their hour was at hand but when they approached Troy in force it seemed to recede before them, dust clouds rising up to hide it, its defenders as insubstantial as ghosts, their arrows biting out of the churning whiteness. The more insistent Argives ploughed on ahead, isolating themselves, and I gave them what they'd have found soon enough.

Poseidon found me by the breakers in the moon's darkness. "How long will this go on?" he asked, redolent of cold and brine.

"This?" I asked.

"This war," he said, "this war you are dragging out past all reason."

"The issue is complex."

"From what I've heard, it's tolerably simple."

"Is it? It must be simple indeed, to be so clear to you." It was a cloudless night but the sky crawled with lightning, showing him my face, and he took a step back. Thunder reverberated down the beach.

"Mortal squabbles aren't worth my time," he said, departing.

In the end, the city couldn't be saved. I'd known from the start that I was only buying time but still it pained me to watch the Trojans drag the horse within the walls, the great gate swing silently open, the ancient houses kindle, the Greeks rush in. They prowled the streets with knives and torches, more wolves than men, and the Trojan womens' prayers rose up with the smoke of their dying city, imploring my mercy, and though I pitied them, I did nothing, for I'd gone away, walking on an island without a name where waves roared on a barren beach and I practiced what to say to him.

In a tide pool I saw the tension in my jaw and the battle-light in my eyes—I had the look of a raptor about to dive—so I laid down my arms and armor and stood there in linen, groping for sweetness. I was all elbows and knees, naked without my sword, but embarrassment would do better than a murder-face. Penelope scowled up at me from the water, then Helen, and, for an instant, Aphrodite, but even in war there's a time for honesty. I put an orchid in my hair, trying to get it to stay with fingers that had turned thick and clumsy; there must, I thought, be an art to it.

While Troy burned and the Greeks rioted Odysseus was in his black ship getting ready to go home. I watched him work from the shadows of the creaking hold, drawing out the moment, foolishly happy just to look at him. When I finally appeared he smiled, noticed my bare shoulders and empty hands, and started drawing inferences. I was committed.

He valued eloquence, but my speech came out in a rush. I offered him everything. He listened, chin on hand, nodding, looking away from me, like I was explaining a plan he needed to remember.

When I finished there was a pause, and my life seemed to be hanging by a thread, and then he laughed in my face.

I am the terror of heaven. Swift thinking. Giant-breaker. Queen of citadels. Deluded in judgment. Risible to men. Worthless to heroes. Widely despicable. I thought of the vast emptiness of the sea, of mountains undulating endlessly, of the silences there, of the darkness settling over the world. I could have killed him in an instant—he's fragile, as all men are fragile, though I think he doesn't know it, but instead I embraced him, and kissed him, once, and didn't kiss him again, and then I vanished.

.

I sat on the beach as his ship raised anchor, dwindled, disappeared, and soon all the Greeks were gone, leaving only a few dispirited Trojans lurking in their city's ruin. They saw me sometimes, and called me the white lady of the dunes. The wind brought rumors of his suffering but I didn't move—he would have thought I was still trying, that he had abased my pride, that I was no warrior, that I was nothing more than a woman in love. So I sit here through the seasons' turning, motionless, watching the sea.

5

PANOPTICON

Circe was a witch and the daughter of the sun. She had the gift of prophecy. Odysseus bested her and became her lover. Medea was her niece.

Dawn finds me on my island's highest eminence, watching my father's rays redden the world. The air is of such clarity and my gaze so piercing that I see every stone and blade of grass on the islands laid out below me like a map; miles away, the mainland is equally visible; through my father's gift of prophecy, so is the future. My eyes scan over the sea and finally settle on lovely Scylla bathing her long limbs in a saltwater pool. Glaukos watches her from a cliff-top but if she sees him she gives no sign unless she moves the more languidly, aware of how her skin glows like sun on wet sand. Tomorrow, Glaukos will despair and sail to Aiaia where he'll climb the long stairs to my high house and beg me to use my power to help him win her. My voice carefully level, I'll ask how can she refuse him when she isn't as fair as him, not as fair by half, at which he'll look blank and say she smiles when he ventures to kiss her, suffers him for a moment, then runs away laughing. I'll frown like a thunderhead and say he shouldn't waste himself on her, for isn't *my* beauty greater, and besides I'm immortal, and in any case I know all, at which he'll stammer that he hadn't meant to, that he'd merely intended . . . Before he can start the long voyage home I'll fly through the air to Scylla's mirror-clear pool and in secret night defile it with a dreadful poison that will make a horror of her beauty, and the burgeoning of her long necks and shrieking misery and unappeasable hunger will in some way be a prologue to the suffering of Odysseus, who isn't yet born, some of whose men will die in her gullets decades from now as the tide of his disasters bears him toward my island. Forewarned of me, he'll counter my witchery with *moly* and demand that I swear by Styx not to harm him as I watch him watching me with the tip of his sword-blade thrilling the skin above my jugular. We'll love briefly and then he'll go back to the sea, and though much of this will be my own doing, all of this is inevitable, and for all my wisdom I don't know why I'll act as I will act, or who I am.

6

SCYLLA

Scylla was a sea-nymph of great beauty. Circe's magic made her a monster. Later, she devoured many of Odysseus' crewmen.

I haunt the shallow waters. Glaukos is on the shore with the other youths and maidens, among whom I once was. They lie in the sun and wade carelessly in the surf. I pass long hours below the waves, watching the sun gleam on their bodies as the salt waves surge under them, lift them up, dissolve on the shore. If they see me, they think I'm a shadow on the seafloor.

I, too, was beautiful once. So much so that every morning Glaukos hid on a cliff overlooking the sea pool where I bathed, delighting in the warm water, the horizontal light, the ardor of his gaze. I wanted him, but there was time enough, and I never let him touch me. When? he asked. Tomorrow, I said. Tomorrow and tomorrow and tomorrow without end.

I knew I played the coquette, but it's a short

road from love to a mother's cares, and I was jealous of my beauty. I waited too long, and now my beauty is gone (though sometimes I think it hasn't gone but only changed, that it survives in the elastic grace of my roiling necks, in the sickle-moon gleam of my innumerable teeth).

When I find him he's floating at the break-line, blueness bleeding from his eyes onto his sun-burned face. I reach out and grasp him—his skin is thin, as mine was once thin, and easily pierced—and pull him toward me as the rip recedes. He thrashes, but I won't let go. I hold him close for a long time, but he won't speak to me, as no one now speaks to me. His luminous flesh becomes dull limbs bobbing uselessly.

I let the current take us. We drift out to sea. The waning day, the island's fading lights. Twilight, and the island a black smear on the horizon; the water is deep here—this is the place. I sigh, and give him the kiss he once begged of me, and let him fall into the swell, the fathoms black below him; his dead eyes watch me as he falls, and his hands reach up, as though he's remembered some final thing, and then he's lost in dark water.

I lift up my voices and shatter the night with my emptiness, my heartlessness. With nothing now to bind me, the world is a hunting ground.

NOCTURNE

Elpenor sailed with Odysseus.

The solitude was balm to him. The other soldiers had never been kind; the camp had been unbearable, even worse than the enforced intimacy of the ship.

Here, all was starlit and silent. He lay sprawled on the roof of the stone house, the slate still warm, as it was always warm, and kept watch on the blank, murmuring ocean. Now and then he heard women's voices in the rooms below but they never approached.

Restless, he clambered down the house's rough stones and set out into the island's empty hills. Somewhere in the wood a wolf fell into step beside him, its ears flicking at every creaking branch and groaning trunk, and he was glad of the company. Finally it yawned, sniffed the air, and padded off into the brush.

High in the hills he found the jagged teeth of a

broken wall around the remnants of a city. The ruin seemed watchful, as though it were contemplating the sky, lost in long architectural thoughts. He stopped to listen to the wind surge through the trees and vales and then fall off, as though gathering itself for a final blast that never came.

From a hilltop he saw a distant river. He thought he saw men's silhouettes on the water's reflected luminance. The river never seemed to come closer but then he came out of a mist and it was right before him. A blind old man sitting on a stone looked up at him with sightless eyes and said, "You're lost. Go on, my dear—your way lies there," and pointed across the river into the dark. He stood there considering the black water, but the wind-troubled night oppressed him, and finally he turned back.

It was still dark when he saw the house again, but he couldn't remember when last he saw the sun. Among the trees and shadows behind the house was a body long dead, the flesh long since turned to leather, the chiton rags and dust. He pitied this hapless victim who lacked the rites of burial and must wander as a restless ghost, but the emotion was abstract and the dust he lifted slipped through his fingers, so once again he picked his way up over the rough stones onto the high roof, the smooth slate familiar under his hands, and perched on the edge, knees clasped to his chest, drinking in the silence.

AJAX

Ajax was a Greek hero who fought in the Trojan War. He was as strong as Achilles but less brilliant. The gods didn't love him, but no man could beat him, and he survived the war unscathed.

Salamis burned as I ran through the streets roaring like the flames and calling out every man I saw but they receded before me like a fading bad dream and my spear was like a stone in my hand. Morning found me sitting alone in my city's smoking ruin.

Days and nights came and went and the rain cut pale streaks on my blackened hands. I stared up into the night without blinking and watched white stars slide over the sky. When a sail nicked the horizon I hoped that my foe-men had returned for their fallen, but it was only Agamemnon, who saw me and the bodies and the burn and the ruin and his eyes wondered but he asked nothing, saying only that it had come to war, in Mycenae, and I was needed. He started in on a story about a wanton woman fleeing far over the wide water but I sighed and stood, spear over shoulder, and walked down the steep beach to the waiting black ships.

We sailed to Troy beach and saw the surf bursting beneath the white walls of the city and the soldiers teeming black on the shore. The other Greeks scattered from their welcome of arrows but I lifted my shield and stood braced on the prow; the swift arrows sang a high death song around me and only fell silent when the keel cut sand. I jumped into the swell and was first up the white beach and the sword-web of battle felt like coming home. I felt fear in the foe-men as my spear dowsed for heart's blood, and as I made wretched widows I was ready to die, but no blade would bite me and soon they went running and I leaned on my spear as kites blackened the sky. They said I'd been screaming over the great din of battle but I remembered no more than the silence behind the clash of weapons and the faces of the men I'd killed. They built a beachhead as the fallen were gathered and the blackness that had lifted came back and remained.

That night I gulped raw wine from great jars while others sat talking, then left for the strand and stared at the waves. The hard crash of the salt sea meant as little as Helen, but the war waged to win her would give shape to my days. No clouds in the fading sky, and I thought of the rain, come late to my country, how hard the ground was when I dug my wife's grave, how she'd made a game once of mocking my grimness, and perhaps would again when I saw her in Hell.

Every time I walked over the white sand toward the shining Trojan host I thought, *Perhaps it will be today.* There was an eerie calm on the battlefield, and the Trojans' spears and swords seemed to move slowly, wounding only the air as I slipped aside and like a good craftsman I worked through their lives. When I felt the Greeks waver I'd call them all to me and we'd fight on as brothers as I pushed through the fray. Death, I knew, was close at hand, and I called him out, but he never came.

In the beginning of the war I sat at other men's fires and tried to be one of them but there was a lightness in their raillery I could never match and my silence was so deep they lost their words and sat staring till I rose and went away. I heard them talking about me, how they valued my strength but thought I was brutal, a spreading black stain on the bright dream of war, and after that I stayed inside my tent, the walls snapping and shivering in the wind, and never took off my armor. When I looked inside the shadows of my helm in my dented bronze mirror I saw only a void and a darkness, which I recognized as my true face, obscured till I'd learned to live solely for strife.

Years passed, and the war wound on, ranks of soldiers rising and falling like the crashing white waves, and every day was the same, and some men died, and others stopped caring. Life had the texture of a nightmare unending but I'd embraced the horror and it made me untouchable. The others thought I was bad luck because I laughed at odd times, and sometimes

I forgot where I was, and sometimes on the field I thought I was in some other battle, any battle at all.

I was nearby when Achilles disappeared. I heard the ecstasy in the Trojans' voices and came roaring through the churning white dust to find his empty bronze armor rolling on the ground. I threw myself against the Trojans and held them at spear's length while Odysseus seized the armor, and, finding it heavy, dragged it away.

It had seemed the war would last forever and I'd be fighting for the rest of my days but the death of Achilles shocked events into motion and it wasn't long before Memnon had drunk deep of death and silver-tongued Odysseus had smuggled us into the city in his creaking invention and then it was just hours till Troy was burning and I was running through the streets with a sword in each hand, mute, beyond myself, killing everyone, and even the other Greeks fled from me; the world was the color of blood and the last thing I remembered was pressing Cassandra's face into Athena's marble altar as I pushed my sword into her neck.

I woke in the morning in the ruins of someone's bedroom, sticky with blood, still clutching a sword, and walked back toward camp through the burned-out city. Everything was over, and nothing was left. Every morning for weeks I went and stood alone in my armor on the abandoned field, staring up blankly at Troy's ruined walls. Once I saw Hector's ghost among the dust devils, and called out to him, but he was looking out to sea, and when I approached he dissolved on the wind.

The allies soon left us, and then the other Greeks were loading their ships and it was time for last things. We stood in a circle as Agamemnon praised our valor and distributed spoil to the strongest in war. The little men got the horses and tripods but the great prize was Achilles' armor, god-forged and golden, doomed to go home with the best warrior of all. When it was the only prize left I stepped forward to claim it but Odysseus looked at Agamemnon, who said the choice lay with the men.

After me the best of the Greeks were Odysseus and Diomedes; Diomedes spoke first. "Fleet as the gods am I," he boasted, "and relentless as water. Joyful I run to the red strife of war."

I said, "Strongest of soldiers, I hold hard the long line, and make heroes run headlong who do not yearn to die. Fleet are the fearful who flee from the war-fray; to walk will suffice for a man seeking war."

Odysseus shook his head and said, "What speed and what strength—you two are truly incredible! I won't even try to compete with such paragons, for, beggar that I am, I have no better gift than wisdom, and who but a fool would see fit to try? The simple truth is that I honor you both, as a chess-master honors chess-men, whose mute, simple courage is the heart of the game." He went on from there, likening himself to an architect and us to his workmen, or his donkeys, and the men laughed, and then I stopped listening until they started applauding and I looked up to see Achilles' golden helmet in Odysseus' soft hands.

No one slept that night, and the camp was full of quarrels and drunken shouting as I sat thinking of my city's ruin across the bitter cold sea. I needed a war but Greece was exhausted, the men keen to return to fields gone rank. I fell asleep thinking of weeds sprouting among my city's wrecked walls and fallen towers, and doubting I'd live long enough to see them remade.

Deep in the night I opened my eyes when I realized there was a war for the taking, and right at hand. I armed myself in silence; the muddy roads through the camp glowed white in the moonlight and luck must have been with me because I met no one on the way to Odysseus' tent. In the absence of his eloquence, I thought, the army will support me, and if they don't, I've always meant to have my tomb here.

At first I thought it was a warrior standing before his tent but then saw it was a woman, though very tall, leaning on her spear and glaring at me, her armor ancient, her helm glittering like the sea. I was going to brush past her but saw the hell-light in her eyes and from the way she held her spear I knew she could use it. I dodged her first thrust by instinct and with joyful disbelief realized that here at last was a worthy enemy, better even than Hector; we faced off in the moonlight, spears poised, waiting, watchful of openings, achingly aware of the empty space between us. A noise from Odysseus' tent and I felt her concentration waver, but my spear missed her heart and I realized she'd been drawing me in, and as I twisted away from her riposte I lost my balance and blundered into the tent. Entangled in its folds I felt something pierce my side, and when I finally threw off the enveloping cloth I found myself on the steep sandy bank of a black river in flood.

The undulating black hills never reach the sea, but just keep going on, and the sun never rises, and even the next hill seems indefinite, no more than a suggestion of dark mass and curvature.

There are others on the slopes, staring into the distance, but I approach no one until I see my wife standing on a hillside. I crush her shoulder in my hand and she turns and looks up at me but nothing moves in her face as I say, *I missed you, and I needed you, and I moved upon the earth to little purpose after you died.* Finally my words seem to register and she smiles faintly but it soon fades and her gaze slips away into the distance.

There's nothing left then, but I keep walking, and time passes, and passes, and then someone is polluting the shadows with his breath and hot blood. "Ajax!" says Odysseus, who is still, it seems, among living men. He says, "Is it you? My friend, it's good to see you, even in this dismal place, though a bitter fate found you. Tell me—how did you die, and what is news of the land of the dead?" but I turn away and walk on into the dark.

9

CUMULUS

Odysseus visited many cities. Some said he never stopped wandering.

The brightness blinding Odysseus' eyes resolves into banks of incandescent thunderheads. He blinks, and averts his gaze from the noon glare, his eyes sliding down over the glowing cloud mass that grades imperceptibly into the battlements of white towers and curtain walls that rise above weather-vanes, the red imbricated tile, the wrought-iron balconies looming over the mazy turns of the street where he stands as strangers rush around him.

There is a temple before him, rippling as though in a heat haze. He peers within but its gods' shining faces are strange to him, and even as he watches the temple dissolves, its domes, pediments, pillars melting and flowing into another order, and now there are alcoves where altars were and the capitals support a frieze showing gods pursuing nymphs becoming stags, stones, trees, wells, water.

Odysseus accosts a passerby and says, "O stranger, speak plainly to a man without a home, and tell me the name of this city."

The stranger says, "Know, O wanderer, that this is the city where islands of apparent order are ellipses in an endless flux, where the elements of architecture forever dissolve and recombine. As it is with the city, so it is with the citizens—even heroes. Once the sea brought a master mariner, whose mind was like a city full of twists and turns; he's long gone now, but survives in the sporadic flights of eloquence one hears in the market-place, and in the labyrinthine complexity of our streets. Sometimes one still hears his name—*Odysseus*."

10

ARACHNE

Arachne was an artist of great talent. She was Athena's only female protégé. When they fell out, Arachne hanged herself.

When the rope tightened and the world turned grey I expected to see nothing, or perhaps Death's opening white hands, but instead Athena was there, lifting me up to relieve the pressure on my neck, and she'd become a giant, so vast she held me on the palm of her hand. I looked up into her face and saw pity, but then the image fractured into elements without meaning, a fissure where her mouth had been, her eyes blue suns.

Now I live in her garden, though I rarely think of her, and I work all the time. I have my designs, in lieu of my life, and I weave and re-weave them through endless iterations, honing their purity, symmetry, radial lines.

11

CALYPSO

Calypso was a sea-goddess, exiled in the war that brought the gods to power. Odysseus washed up on her island, stayed for years, and then left.

She sits where he once sat on her island's one hill. Cloud shadow moves over her, the sun burns behind white massifs and the sea shifts through gradients of light. He was looking for anyone, but she's looking only for him. He's been gone a long time now, but still she looks for his white sail to nick the horizon, for then it won't be long until he runs laughing through the shallows to embrace her and tell her that he's raised his son, buried his wife, left all his lands in order, all that is proper in a mortal man, and now he's done, and has come back to her. But the sun sinks, the day fades, and his ship, if there were a ship, would be invisible.

Her eyes close, in the sun's heat, and she dreams of swimming in a sea as red as blood, and as warm, and then she dreams of nothing.

Hours pass, or centuries.

Waking, the clouds are gone and the sand has all but interred her. The roots of rank orchids are tangled in her hair; she rises in a cascade of sand and broken flowers. She hears a new note in the surf, sees the breakers boiling whiter where the reef has grown. She swims in the sea, salt water washing her, and sees the same scuttling crabs in their blue shells and the same flitting incurious fishes.

There had been stumps from the timbers he felled but now they've become a thicket. His raft left a scar as it slid down the hill but now she can only find the old furrow by touch. She finds his axe where he dropped it, entombed in moss; she shivers, when she sees it, and her mind goes dark as she picks it up and flings it end over end toward the sea.

He'd said he was a prisoner on Ogygia. He was with her all of seven summers. She's been on Ogygia since the seas were cold and there were other constellations in the night sky. There'd been a long, cruel war, and her father had been on the losing side—he'd risked all and lost all and she was lost with him. She remembers Hermes' hard fingers crushing her wrist as he hauled her through the sky to the island of her exile. "When can I go home?" she'd asked, but he'd said nothing as he turned and went away.

On her hill watching the sea she thinks of the axe again, the way his hands' sweat had mottled the haft. She leaves her vigil to swim in the blue water in the reef's circle and by afternoon she's found it, wave-stirred in the white sand below the surging water. The haft is coral-scarred now, and the blade corroded, but it's intact, and she puts it back on the hill among the trees.

He could, she reminds herself, be cruel. He barely listened when she spoke of the sea-shifts through the centuries, of the other islands she'd known. He professed to hate her, called her witch and jailer, but had he not come to her bed each night, and is it so difficult to lie on the cold earth alone?

Her cave has filled with sand, her linen turned to rot, her loom disintegrated. She no longer bothers to dress, and has turned as brown as the nereids who sometimes pass by. Sisters, she calls, what news? What have you heard of Odysseus? They rise up in the waves, smile at her, shake their heads unknowingly.

One night there's a storm. She sits in the wind-torn wood and sees a ship rush through the moonlight like a desperate ghost. It strikes on the reef, masts and sails collapsing in a tangle of rigging and then a great wave buries it in foam. Sailors wash up in the morning, and she drags their bodies above the water-line, washes the salt away, buries them in damp loam. There's one, she finds, who's still breathing, so she exhumes her old bed in the cave and puts him in it, plies him with healing drugs, holds him tight as he shivers and sweats, but on the fourth night he dies without having spoken and she washes his body and buries him with his friends.

She goes back to her vigil. The sun is hot. Her eyes close. When she wakes the island is more verdant and the sea has risen higher on its shores. Athena is sitting beside her, and for once her raptor's eyes are kind. "Your exile is over," Athena says. "The war has been forgotten by victor and vanquished alike, and Odysseus isn't coming back. You're free now. You can move on." Calypso's eyes stay on the horizon, and she gives no sign of having heard. Eventually Athena leaves her.

PART III

ZEUS

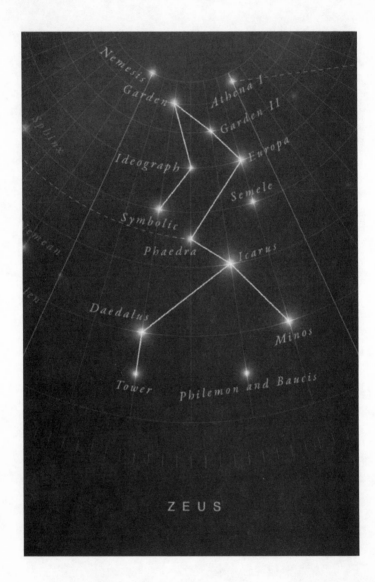

ZEUS

12

NEMESIS

Older than the gods, Nemesis brought the proud low. Zeus was her enemy.

Nemesis unfurled her black wings and blotted out the stars, and I was elated, for my rage had lacked an object, but she must have thought better of challenging me because she turned into light falling away into the void.

For aeons I'd felt stultified and done nothing but watch the passing waves of radiation, the whorling nebulae, the evolving order of the stars. There'd been wars, I think, in which I'd been the victor, but even then they were far in the past. I knew Nemesis was an inimical power out of old night but I threw myself after her.

I became a black sun massive enough to bend space and trap light along with millions of stars but out among them I saw her become a moon so I became a planet to bind her in my orbit.

She became ice, miles thick, entombing me, but I

became a fire in the planet's core, my flame pouring forth from the planet's crust to fill its atmosphere with gas, heat-trapping, ice-melting.

There are gaps after that, though I've put great effort into reconstructing our duel. I have few certainties, but I do know she was always in retreat, or seemed to be, and I remember glimpsing her through a thousand fathoms of water, and how it felt to become a shark, but sharks haven't changed in two hundred million years, so I can't put a time to that moment.

Toward the end I chased her over the world's surface. Her play had been degenerating, it seemed— elegant countermoves were a thing of the past, and in her last score of transformations she'd become monstrous animals hiding in the forests while I pursued her as a hero with a gleaming blade in my hand; it had come to seem natural to course after her through terrestrial woods and it gave me pause to remember where I was from.

I finally ran her to ground on a mountaintop in Attica. I'd seen her slowing and knew it was time for the *coup de grâce* so I became a lord with lightning in his hand at which she became a woman of great beauty. I took this for mere perversity, and thought her goal was to die elegantly, but as I raised my hand to finish her I finally noticed her total absence of fear and then once again she unfurled her black wings and blotted out the world.

"Everything was yours," she said. "But you let me draw you in. Now look at you. You're little more than a man, with a man's appetites and a man's weaknesses, and you'll squander the centuries on mortal loves and wars. What you were is lost for good, and I did it, *I*."

Then she was gone. I cast the bolt anyway but it snarled harmlessly through empty air.

That was long ago, and I haven't seen her since. Now I sit on my throne on Olympus, watching the sky, trying to remember.

13

ATHENA I

Athena was Zeus' daughter and his favorite. She sprang fully formed from his dream of the world.

Cumuli dissolve in the deep blue below the stark throne where Zeus sprawls dreaming. Images of shadowed caves, ancient mountains, giants' animosity grade into the tangled limbs of past lovers, their fragrant skin, its friction, but behind this there's a sadness and an absence that stays with him even as the dream dissolves into an awareness of all the islands scattered on the sea and the sweat slick on his brow.

His lightning pulses in the quiver by his throne, its coruscation a reminder of the days of skies smothered in black smoke and the holocaust of primeval enemies but his gaze moves out into the gulf of air over the empty sweep of ocean where glass-smooth waves in serried ranks slide across the water toward an island of white sand where a tower rises among the breakers, and there at its apex is a woman staring at the sky. Clouds uncover the sun and she squints into the light as it brightens into brilliance and illuminates the planes of her face; the surf explodes against the tower then, and in the concussion and clattering water's fall he's there with her. She struggles, at first, but his force and his heat are as stupefying as summer and her will dissolves like a sand-bank in the tide, but even as her ripped tunic pools on the ground his joy has faded. Her pale body, he sees, is just another link in the endless chain of his tepid mortal amours, and his eyes turn to the hard glare on the sweep of sea, the vacant sky, and then he's rising up in eagle-shape, and below him the woman, the tower and then the island dwindle and vanish.

He circles idly on the thermals above the shadows of the low clouds scudding over the sea, leviathans breaching in the bright spaces between them, and there in the distance is the loom of the land and in the high dry hills above the sea a maiden chases her own shadow, javelin gleaming in her hand, and in her gait and the lines of her body are a pride and a ferocity that make him drift closer and then bank and hurtle down through the air. When she crests the hill he's waiting for her, wearing the shape of her sister, lying in the shade of an oak. The hunt is long, he calls to her, the heat longer, so why not lie with her in the shade through the worst of the afternoon? The girl stands in the sun, body streaming, considering, and then she casts down her weapon and sprawls in the prickling grass, and only a moment later she's clawing at his eyes as she fights to get away; her teeth pierce his hand and in momentary pain he uses all his strength and she collapses, her breath crushed out. Blood wells from her mouth and runs down her cheek, and her eyes won't focus, and he can see that she wants to die but she takes her will in her hands and opens her shaking arms to him, for to invite isn't quite to be defeated.

He thinks of the distant season of his youth, the apocalyptic violence of the sons of the Earth, the storms that churned the oceans and shook the world and how he'd kept fighting when no one had much expected him to live. The girl on her back below him seems like nothing so much as a terrified young animal. Do it, she slurs, but he shakes his head and turns away from her as a fog settles over the hills and as he walks his eyes are full of migraine light. Sand underfoot, and ocean before him, and as he wades through the fog into the water the island vanishes.

He forges through the waist-deep water holding his head in his hands thinking the days will bring no more than empty loves repeated. Waves break on his chest, surge over his head, and the numbing cold is welcome even as his vision blurs and his head throbs, and then on a spur of black rock before him is a woman, naked, sleeping on her side, and he sees her with such clarity that the rest of the world seems to fade. Smooth curve of white thigh, and as he approaches he feels the heat from her skin; her jaw is tense, her fingers curl, and she seems to dream of battle. He leans over her, looking her in the face, poised to touch her, but in that moment she opens her eyes, which are bright, grey and hard, and he seems to see them with more than ordinary clarity as she drives her palmed stone into his skull.

Blackness, and the washed-out after-image of her

eyes, and somewhere blood is pouring down his face, diffusing in the sea, and then the plunk as she drops the stone into the water. It would be easy to let go and drift but he rises up out of the water and wipes the blood from his eyes in time to see her launch into the air in the shape of a gull.

He follows as an eagle and they race over the water faster than arrows or wind and then they rise up through a churning storm's strata and in the tumult of rain and cloud he loses her. Then a gap in the white shows her streaking toward his mountain and in that moment her plan is clear to him. He chases her in earnest then, miles flickering by in moments as they fly over the flanks and then the slope of Olympus and then at the mountain's apex she's a woman again as she reaches for the lightning that arcs and shudders in its quiver by his throne. He lunges for her, and his fingers brush her heel as her hand closes around the incandescent bolt, and then she's facing him with the lightning raised high and her eyes full of murder, and for the first time since the morning of the world he takes a step back.

Zeus puts a good face on things, calling her his daughter and his lightning-bearer, and she plays her part gracefully, giving good counsel among the great gods. He loves her most of all his children, for all that she gives him no repose (he never looks at the flash of thigh above her greaves, at the white span of neck below her helmet), and at times he wants to forget her, but she's never far from his mind.

14

EUROPA

Zeus kidnaped Europa from the shores of Phoenicia in the form of a white bull. He left her on Crete.

In the last of the light we gather white flowers from the vines twisted deep in the roots of the dunes. A wall of black cloud blots the light in the west as the rising wind stirs our hair, and there in the surf's tumult is a white bull, foam surging and receding around his legs, stirring the sea-wrack that hangs from his neck. We converge on this apparition speechlessly, though in the distance the maids are calling us already, and the sun is almost gone, and soon they'll be lighting the fires and closing the doors and locking them against the night. The bull's horns are as long as our forearms, but it stands peacefully in the tide-race, waiting, and I step forward alone to crown him with white flowers. Heart pounding, I put my hand on his flank, and his heat is radiant through the sea-cold. He turns and looks out to sea and I know he's about to leave. Wait, I say, as he wades into the surf, and my dress pools around my hips as I wade after him, shivering already, and he hesitates for just a moment, but that's enough for me to wrap my arms around his neck.

He can only walk out so far, I reason, but then he's swimming, and when I look back the other girls are standing at the surf-line watching, not even waving as he heaves against the rip and a wave washes over us and bears the flowers away.

The storm rises, black and howling, and the bull is swimming faster now, the shore lost behind me, and in the chaos of night and water the only thing to do is press my face into his hide. Time becomes motion and cold and the animal beneath me, and my strength is failing when the wind's moan subsides and the bull is walking up out of the surf onto a beach before cliffs implied by gradations in the shadows and there's no one there at all. I roll down onto the sand, stagger, and sit hugging my knees. I only mean to close my eyes but when I wake it's dawn, the bull vanished, the pale light revealing this long expanse of beach, the black inland mountains, my freedom, this emptiness.

15

IDEOGRAPH

Cadmus went searching for his kidnaped sister Europa. In compensation for having taken her, Zeus granted him a boon. Cadmus wanted what he wrote to become real. Zeus agreed, with the condition that he had to be exact.

When Cadmus inscribed Europa's name in the desert sand she rose like a mirage before him, but he grieved to find she was a mere pallid abstraction, her features vague, partaking neither of life nor history.

That was years ago, but Cadmus is still there, writing out the details of her bitten fingernails, the shadows in the basements of their father's house, the salt-stains on her dress, how she'd watched him play in the surf while she waited for something to happen, staring out to sea as her mind wandered . . .

16

SYMBOLIC

As Cadmus' brush touches the blank white sheet the door to his study bursts open and a stranger enters, trembling. Cadmus doesn't look up from his work as the stranger draws breath and says, "Listen to me. I, too, was a calligrapher once. Diligent in practice, I drew every intricate stroke of the character *symbolic* a thousand thousand times." He pauses for a moment and Cadmus regards him silently, his brush poised, resuming his work as the stranger continues, "The shape of every line is the product of countless accidents— weave of paper, wear of bristles, the tremor in my hand—and each is, or should be, unique.

"Mine were identical—spatter for spatter, stroke for stroke. I realized I'd been writing not a character but the idea of a character.

"It follows that the world is false, a coarse and empty calculus of symbols, a line in the script of some demiurge, who, through laziness or parsimony, is not thorough in his work. In his carelessness, I surmised, he might have left a door ajar that should have been shut. It's been a long way but I found that door, and now, finally, I'm here, and you must tell me what the world is."

Still writing, Cadmus asks, "What's your name?"

The stranger says, "Some name—I don't remember!"

Cadmus asks, "How did you come here?"

The stranger says, "Some road—I don't know!"

Cadmus draws his guest's attention to the page he has been writing; on it is a single, simple character, much of its interior empty, its architecture built around the voids. As he adds the last strokes, he says, "You learned that there is no character, just the few wisps of meaning in the idea of a character. Had your doubt gone further you might have known yourself, my skeptic, my parable, my symbol among symbols, but then you would stand for something else."

17

SEMELE

Semele was the daughter of Cadmus, the first king of Thebes. Zeus became her lover, saying he was a mortal king but always visiting her in the dark. When Zeus' wife Hera discovered the affair she disguised herself as Semele's maid and suggested that her lover was low-born; she advised Semele to make her lover swear to reveal himself, and to press him on his oath three times.

She'd promised herself she'd lock her door but leaves it ajar. Waiting, she feels like she's only ever been a woman waiting for her lover in the dark.

Eventually she feels the air move as the door silently opens. There's the sense of pressure she always feels when he comes to her, and then his hand finds her shoulder and pulls her in.

"Wait," she says, and has a sense of his incredulity. "First grant me a favor."

"Anything," he says, a grin in his voice. "I swear by Styx."

"I've never seen your face," she says. "You say you're a king, but you might be no one, so tell me who you really are."

"In fact, I am a king," he says, "and one greater in dignity than your husband, so set your heart at rest." He pulls her closer but she turns her face away from his and says, "You haven't really told me who you are."

"Very well," he says, and his voice is different now, filling the room and vibrating in her bones. "I am cloud-gatherer and storm-king, lord of lightning and the upper air, Zeus, Cronos' son."

His strength is irresistible but even so she says, "You still haven't told me who you really are."

His hands relax and let her go. There's a moment of silence, and then he says, "In fact, I'm no one, or very nearly. I'm the strongest, and I carry the lightning, and I remember a few things from the early days, but beyond that there's nothing much at all, just these few attributes and a handful of stories."

She finds herself pitying him. She reaches up to touch his face and says, "Tell me the stories."

"In one, Zeus becomes the lover of a princess of Thebes by pretending to be a mortal king, and though he comes to her every night, she's never seen his face. His wife Hera discovers the affair and takes the shape of the princess's old nurse to make her wonder whether some man of low rank is exploiting her. She persuades the princess to press her lover to reveal himself three times in succession."

"And then?"

"He honors his oath, though he has a kindness for her."

Now there's nothing under her hand. She says, "How does the story end?"

"Full of regret, he returns to his dream of the world. As for her, she was never much at all, no more than the barest outline of the feminine, a querulousness, and a sense of waiting in the night. At the end of the affair she vanishes."

18

PHAEDRA

Phaedra was the daughter of Minos and Pasiphae and the granddaughter of Europa. Theseus killed her half-brother Asterion, who was also called the Minotaur. Theseus then seduced her sister Ariadne, whom he later abandoned.

Theseus' son Hippolytus was beautiful.

I sat up blinking, drowning, fending off Ariadne as she shook me awake, but then she said once again that she wasn't coming back. "Find me in Athens when you can," she said, "and until then goodbye," and before I could find words she ran away into the dark.

I reached the hall in time to see her white night-gown disappearing. I'd often spied on her in the white hills, brooding on the walls, lying with her young men on the beaches, but I was still half asleep and stumbling and the palace was like a dense confusion of cold wind, low whispers, servants peering myopically from corners, and I soon lost her. I stood there listening, trying to intuit her trajectory, then found the thread in the distant echoes of her steps which I followed to the labyrinth, but its foyer was empty, the moonlight shining on the mosaic of the bull carrying a girl over the sea, and then the labyrinth's bronze doors opened.

There emerged a boy of pale, lupine beauty, and in his hand he held a knife as long as his forearm that seemed to gather in all the light. The sun rose in my chest as I saw the black blood staining his hands and arms and I couldn't look away from the blade which he turned in his hand so the moonlight rippled on the watermark. He stepped toward me, poised, but I couldn't seem to move or focus on anything but the knife. Ariadne rushed in then, white face flushed and blue eyes streaming as she flung her arms around him like a drowning sailor grasping a spar.

As my sister sobbed into his neck he watched me over her shoulder, impassive, his eyes catching the light the way the knife did, and I saw him decide. "Your people," he said in a surprisingly gentle mainland voice, "they aren't so good. Maybe you won't be like them," as Ariadne wept the harder. His eyes were cold as he stroked her neck and I could see him wondering how long he had to hold her, and I wanted to warn her, but I knew she wouldn't listen, and finally he saluted me with the knife and led her away.

From the battlements I watched their ship on the lightening sea, white sails fading into blue of distance.

•

I went to my bedroom and burrowed into the bed-clothes. When I woke it was full light and someone was hammering on my door; Ariadne has been kidnaped, they cried, and Theseus has escaped, and Asterion is dead.

Poseidon's temple flickered with firelight as the surging flames of the funeral pyre consumed Asterion's great body. We stood watching as the fire burned down to coals, his long, blackened horns protruding from the ashes.

That night I dreamed of lightless, echoing rooms where a massively horned shadow sat alone in the dark. He smelled like horses and old iron and blood, and gave no sign of noticing me until in a small voice I said, "Aren't you lonely here?"

"No," he said, his voice vibrating the stones, "for Daedalus has told me of the world without, and it, too, is a prison and a maze without end. Here, at least, the walls are tangible. In any case, I've learned that my old home was only the least of all the antechambers of the vast and intricate labyrinths of Hell."

The day after the funeral my father was unnaturally cheerful, striding through the palace clasping shoulders and slapping backs, though I'd never known him to touch anybody. He couldn't stop talking about the invasion of Athens, which, he said, was imminent—he would raze the city, rescue his daughter, mount Theseus' head on a spike. Daedalus, his black-robed engineer, followed behind him like a watchful, disinterested crow.

The slaves said it was bad luck to leave the labyrinth without a center and in fact every week brought more bad news—ships wrecked, colonies burned, our allies turned against us, and as Crete's star tumbled Athens' rose, their ships sweeping the sea-roads clean. From the harbor wall I watched the war-ships' lading, wondering when they'd bring her back, but the few that left never returned.

I wrote letters to my sister and sent them by ships bound for Athens, or for anywhere, like arrows fired into the sky. I wanted to ask her how she could leave me, how she couldn't have foreseen what would happen, but, as anyone might open them, I worded them so carefully their very emptiness became a kind of code. There were no replies, and the sailors told me that she hadn't made it to the mainland, or that Theseus had cut her throat, or that some god took her and tired of her and left her in the desert.

The ships dwindled in the harbor, and rain dripped through the holes in the roof, and the servants left, one by one, unless they were too old to find another place. I heard nothing more of the invasion, and never heard my sister's name except when my father called me

Ariadne by mistake. He seemed to shrink, as the years passed, and to be surprised he could actually lose. He only looked happy when he was playing chess with Daedalus.

One day my father summoned me to his study, where he and Daedalus were drawing a map in black ink. He focused on me with an effort, and as though speaking over a great distance said, "It's time you were married."

I was only fifteen, and it was still years till it was time I was married, but I only said, "To whom?"

"Athens," he said, taking up his pen again.

"*Theseus?*"

My father didn't look up but Daedalus steepled his fingers and embarked on a lengthy explanation involving access to markets, the untimely defection of the Tyrians, the strategic value of the Piraeus, and the ships committed to the war in Rhodes, all of which, he said, made an alliance with Athens unavoidable.

"How could you?" I asked my father.

Surprised, he thought for a moment, then said, "Reasons of state."

I stood on the battlements in the first light of morning, watching the white sails of the ship coming to fetch me.

While we were at sea we could have been going anywhere, and somehow I expected strange islands, empty shores, a journey without an end, but on a starless night a sailor cried out and I looked up to see the lights of a city.

As they led me up the stairs to the Acropolis I realized that there had been a time when I could have changed things—flung myself into the water, run off down an alley, hid myself in Crete's white hills—but that time had passed unnoticed. I wondered if Ariadne had walked up these same steps.

The Acropolis was a high, broad platform full of temples whose boundaries were defined by long lines of torches. There were many people, all of them strangers, but none of them looked at me except a boy who I at first thought was Theseus but he was too young, and too beautiful, and he looked lost. They brought me before a soldier marked by years and war and it was only when he told me how he hoped I'd be happy there that I recognized my sister's lover, my half-brother's killer, my husband-to-be. He seemed more like my father's peer than mine; I felt like an unwelcome guest to whom he had to be polite. Some friend of his came and whispered in his ear; Theseus said we'd tend to the formalities another time, squeezed my shoulder, and left. Before they were out of earshot I heard his friend say I was pretty and ask if Minos had other daughters to sell.

It took an hour to find the chamberlain, and another hour for him to find me a room.

I asked the servants about my sister but no one had ever heard of her. My father sent no letters.

One day in the orangery I saw the boy from that first night. He was shy, but didn't run, and I realized he'd been following me. His name was Hippolytus. He outshone his father's memory, but was unaware of it, and no one seemed to want him.

His tutor drank all day whenever Theseus was off hunting, which was almost all the time, so we were left to ourselves. We spent the summer exploring the palace gardens, the cellars, the odd corners of the city, and every afternoon he fell asleep with his head on my lap.

There was a soldier who was supposed to escort me when I went beyond the city walls but I left him sleeping in the orchards and rode with Hippolytus to the sea. He showed me a steep path that led down to a cove he said he alone knew. We sat together on the sand, grasping our knees, not talking, and then a heat rose in me. He tried to conceal his fear, and didn't pull away as I undressed him, though he did say it was unseemly. He clung to me as I stroked his back; I said it didn't matter, that no one was watching and no one cared, that we were past consequences.

19

ICARUS

Icarus was Daedalus' son. He fled Crete on wings his father built.

This continent of cloud so far below me. The curve of the radiant world. These stars burning on a black sky. This silence.

I recollect myself, draw a deep breath, and heave once again against the thin air, the wings my father made me sweeping soundlessly. The world is remote, and the sun flares among the stars in the night sky, its light glaring on my pinions. It's like rising through dark water, and the sun is so bright now it seems close enough to touch. Just a little longer, I tell myself, but there's no goodness in the air, and I can't move my wings.

As my breath fails the constellations blur and though I fight my eyes close, flicker open, close again. I turn my face to the sun and through my eyelids see the red of dawn, or of blood, and then I'm falling.

Dreams of ice floes under polar nights, of stars rising behind glaciers, and of a white bird abandoned to the wind.

I wake in a void. There's no sense of motion, no wind of passage, and I'm finally afraid, not that I'll die but that gravity has failed and I'll float here forever, but then the cloud mass below me has come perceptibly closer, then closer still, and then I'm plunging through rushing white.

Below the clouds the stars have disappeared behind blue skies and the thick air is heady, and then my shoulders burn as I spread my wings to catch the wind. I spiral over an archipelago, then descend toward an island surrounded by even ripples that become waves breaking on white beaches—tumult and churning water, and then I'm staggering through blood-warm breakers, letting them wash over me as I fall onto my back and look up into the sky that's evicted me once again.

The tide goes out, leaving me lying in the warming sand. I unstrap my wings, and my hands trace the broken feathers and singed armature, but it's nothing I can't repair, for I'm my father's son, and soon I'll rise again, and this time touch the sun.

20

MINOS

Minos was king of Crete. Europa was his mother. Daedalus was his oldest friend and the foundation of his power.

The bow creaks as I draw the arrow to my eye. The sun gleams on the whitecaps crawling across the harbor and on the glory of Icarus' broad white wings; he banks, giving me a clear shot, and my arms and the bow are one tension, but I imagine his smooth parabola turned to ragged tumbling and Daedalus' face when he sees his son's body, and hesitate, and the moment passes. As he disappears into the grey fog coming in over the sea I fire my arrow high into the air, pointlessly, and share for a moment his flight's euphoria.

Deep in the labyrinth's mass I stand before the door to Daedalus' cell. The key is in my hand but I'm waiting, listening, for he's the master of artifice and nothing is more probable than that he's vanished with his son, and though I strain to listen there's nothing but a silence that foretells only evil, and then I unlock the door.

I find him bent over his book with his pen in his hand. The little light of the one barred window shows the cell's squalor—the equations scribbled on the walls, the loose papers on the floor, the sour residue of meals pushed into a corner—and the light is at such an angle that I see the black pouches under his eyes, the skin hanging from his face like dessicated silk; he's never looked so old or so weary and I wonder if I've worked him too hard and if he's been sleeping. When he raises his head to look out the window I follow his gaze but see only white cumulus whorling in the wind and below that the sprawling rooftops of the labyrinth, and as though drawn by its complexity my mind turns to its dust and shadows, the white passages and the chambers and the echoing arcades. Mustering myself, I break in on him and say, "Icarus fled Crete today on the white wings you built him. I could have shot him out of the sky, but I held fire, and watched him bank over the waves and vanish into the fog."

Daedalus closes his eyes and then says, "Your Majesty is a gracious king, and I thank you for sparing him."

"The one pair of wings implied another. I searched your workshop and found the second pair."

He smiles and says, "I'm too old for skylarking."

"You're not so old," I say, though he's ten years my senior, and few men my age still go to war.

"The wings were a necessary misdirection—my son only left when he was sure I would follow."

"Your son is less wise than his father."

"My son was right—I'll be gone soon."

"And yet, I prefer that you stay."

"You made my son a hostage, and me a prisoner, so yes, your preferences are clear."

"You're too valuable to let go."

He closes his book, turns to me and says, "Minos, I have served you long enough. I have been the architect of your island and of your wars and of your cities; there's nothing in Crete that does not bear my imprimatur. I made your ships and roads and siege-engines, and I made you a king, though you made me a slave, and now I'm done with you." I can see he's been waiting a long time to say these words and watch him closely, weighing his certainties.

I start to speak but he raises an imperious hand and says, "I am old, and I am sick, and I will die soon. Now that Icarus is free, my one concern is this book," and he holds up the book in which he's been writing, and the day has turned to dusk already and the book's black cover seems to soak up the little light in the small room and he holds it up just a beat too long which lets me know there's something I'm missing. Guessing that the book is a distraction I scan the room for weapons or traps but all that's here are the old man, his bed and the scholar's clutter. "This book is all of me," he says, and his voice has the ring of truth. "It's my soul, my life's work, the sum of my mathematics, the key to the hidden order in the world. I've wasted decades winning your wars, doing my own work in rare stolen hours. My time is short now, though the book is far from done, and soon I will leave you to finish it."

My rage comes close to the surface but I don't lash out because behind my anger is an intuition that somehow he's already gone, though he's right here before me, locked in a cell to which I have the key on the island that's the center of my power. The imminence of his absence howls all around me and I foresee how when he's gone Crete and the palace will be empty shells and there will never again be anyone who knows how things were, and I think of that first night when he came to Crete and we talked till dawn over the roar of the wind of the empire we'd build and of mathematics. I say, "You're not dying, but I'll bring doctors, the best there are. And you can go abroad soon, but just wait a little longer, because for now our kingdom needs you."

"*Our* kingdom is yours, and always has been."

"I've laden you with wealth, and rank, and honor."

"I'm a slave with a golden collar."

"You're Crete's second citizen."

"That distinction, like every distinction craved by your courtiers, is worthless, a complicated way of organizing nothing, as lasting and as valuable as smoke."

The day is failing rapidly and he's faded to planes of shadow and pale light as I say, "Then I'll build you a monument in stone, a colossal statue to stand by the harbor, and every man who sails into Knossos will see your face and know your name. Your fame will be written in granite."

"My face," he says, "is a face like any other, and my name is a noise with no meaning. The only thing about me that deserves to survive, if anything does, is my mathematics, my aesthetic, my way of seeing the world. Faces are drawn in water, and names written in dust. Even persons are ephemeral—in the end, there's only pattern."

"Stay with me," I say, "for there are kings left to conquer, and we'll break them, you and I, and build an altar to our victories from their brittle white bones."

"It would be a monument to vanity and ruin."

"Stay with me," I say, "and I'll give you libraries like gardens, and gardens like labyrinths."

"What's worth reading, I have read. The only book for me now is the one I'm writing."

"Stay with me," I say, "and I'll give you time and silence and solitude. Write your book, and forget the affairs of men and cities. I'll bring you mathematicians, if you want them, the best Hellas has."

"I doubt you'd find another of the kind I need," he says, smiling at me for the first time in as long as I can remember, and once again I feel a secret in the air, and I remind myself that Daedalus' wit has been many strong men's undoing. He says, "You could have been a great mathematician, you know—you have talent, a talent not unlike mine. What a shame you grew into a hard-headed man-of-affairs with no use for mere abstractions." He coughs wetly, and as the evening light fades in the window he's all but invisible though he's right there before me and then in a gentle voice he says, "My friend, you must learn to get along without me. My course is set—I'm going away."

He's my oldest friend, in fact my only one, and he's spent his life building my empire, and to my fathomless disgust my eyes begin to water. Moreover, if I let him go it would mean the end of my wars and so an end to the cries of the dying and the dead eyes of new slaves and the ash and stench of burned-out cities, but I remind myself I'm a man of will, and as the last light disappears I stifle my weakness and say, "The prince you serve will rule the Middle Sea, and that will be me, or that will be no one, and Knossos, which has been your home, is now your prison, and I swear to you, you will die here."

That night I dream of the days when Daedalus and I were never apart and a supplicant knelt not to me but to him, and death was in the supplicant's face when he realized his error but I raised him up and said, "Never mind—he too is Minos," and in the morning my chamberlain wakes me to tell me that Daedalus is gone.

I look for him in the workshops, in the smithies, in the deep tangle of the labyrinth, in dry wells, in oubliettes, in the winding canyons of the inland mountains. I let no ship leave the harbor. I send soldiers to search the towns, huntsmen to set brindled hounds belling through the wood, divers to sink among the reefs. I search the deepest cellars, listen to their silences, look for footprints in the dust. I sit on the beach where we planned our empire the first night he came to Crete, shouting to be heard over the wind; silent now, but for the waves' hiss and lap. In his cell I watch the light fade in his window. He's gone, as are all his papers, leaving nothing but the book.

A darkness settles on my mind and I lack the energy even to stand as my thoughts move sterilely and interminably over the locked gates, the inaccessible beaches, the crenelated towers that should have kept him here. My vacantly circling thoughts bring me no closer to a solution and I catch myself wanting to ask Daedalus for his advice. In the gathering dusk the book seems terrible, its cover a black hole absorbing all the light, and I find I can't look away, as I can't bring myself to touch it, for Daedalus' resource was endless, and he must have hated me, and he had years to give his malice form in spring-loaded needles or poisoned ink or some subtler trap. For a moment I long to burn the book as I once longed to break cities but, having nowhere else to turn, I open it.

When I close the book the one window frames the glow of dawn, or perhaps of dusk, and my mind is full of the forms of clouds, all the shades and gradients of vapor forming ethereal massifs, towering spires, vast

plateaus, and for just a moment I understand the elu-
sive calculus of the upper air, but as I try to hold it in
my mind lucidity becomes confusion and I'm left with
only fragments. I look out the window but the incandescent sky is cloudless, and I'm distantly aware that
I haven't eaten in a long time, and then I go back to
the book.

I'm stifled, drowning, the hard hand of black water
pressing me down; I rise out of the dream with a lurch,
sitting up and knocking my dagger from the desk;
blood streaks my forearm from the wounds on my
wrist where I pricked myself awake. The book lies
open to the page I've read and re-read and dreamed of
re-reading, and once again my eyes go to the ranks of
equations that abstract the crushing weight of water
on the abyssal plains, the way the wind's force on the
surface stirs the cold currents in the deep; the densely
written symbols swim before my eyes, and I know I'll
never understand them, but my heart is a soldier's, so
I blink, steel myself and try again.

Black vault of night and then as the stars fade the sky
lightens until there are only a few lingering planets and
then nothing but swallows arcing after insects through
the morning air over the empty streets. I'm happy, for
it's not far to the center of the city, and all the answers
are there, waiting to be revealed, though they're frag-

ile, and might disperse if I so much as think of them. As I go deeper into the city the walls rise and the light fades, and the street becomes a canyon of uniform planes of shadow, and then I'm feeling my way through lightless, claustrophobic alleys where there's only the pale quadrilateral of colorless sky, the wind's restless octaves, the rough stone under my hands. Then there's a sheer wall before me, and sheer walls all around, and the sky has disappeared, but even so I'm elated because I know the center is close at hand, and then I wake to someone shouting in my ear.

I'm sweating on Daedalus' cot, which still smells of him, clutching the book to my chest, and with relief I recall I'm still many pages from the end. A general watches from the doorway as the minister squatting beside me shakes my arm again and asks me another question but I turn my back on him, pull the blanket tighter, and sleep comes back in a black tide.

When next I wake it's morning and I'm alone. Without rising I open the book and immediately my mind is full of the forms of forked lightning, branched rivers, blood vessels, but I haven't been reading an hour when the writing stops. I flip ahead but the rest of the pages are blank, except for the very last which is covered with scrawled notes, a sort of diary, mostly about his work and the wings he built for his son. The last entry reads: *Minos has a predictable mind, and as of*

now it's a certainty that the book will be finished.
I have one last thing to do, and then I'm gone.

I remember how my generals swore Crete was bound in iron, bound in adamant, that not even a bird now could escape, and I'm on the verge of relieving them first of their commands and then of their lives, but then my rage collapses because the fault was mine, for who but a fool would expect those unremarkable men to contend with Daedalus and his sublimity? I throw the book at the wall, then gather it up tenderly.

He's gone to Athens, I think, that city of chatter and philosophy, where my old enemy Theseus is king and certain to make Daedalus welcome. At first it seems that the only possible plan is to gather my armies and my fleets and commit everything to an invasion first of Athens and then of all Attica and either win a new empire or see all my works destroyed, but armies are slow, while news travels fast, and he'd be gone long before my siege train reached Athens' walls.

That night in the small hours I go to the harbor carrying a bag of gold, a sword, and the book swaddled in canvas. Among the creaking ships I find one whose captain has often served me with discretion. The sentry is asleep on the gunwales; I nudge him with my foot and say, "Wake up. The king has a message for your master." The captain comes on deck in a night-cap, his sleep-blurred face clarifying when he recognizes me, and soon the deck is full of hushed activity and then the sweeps are out and then the sails are filling. As we leave the harbor I watch the city lights and in the receding spattered glow I intuit the presence of a pattern I can't quite articulate.

We sail for days but see no other ships. On the third day we drop anchor an hour before dawn, the shore implied by white breakers and a sense of the land. The Piraeus, the captain says, is two hours' walk north. "Good luck, sir!" he calls as I wade through the warm swell. From the beach I watch faint sails disappearing.

I build a fire and sit with my back to a stone and watch the rising sun define the horizon as I listen to the sea's sizzling blankness. The fire burns low and I let it fade. I've so rarely been alone.

I dream I'm on the battlements of the walls around the harbor watching Daedalus make adjustments to the rows of mirrors that glow like low moons. The harbor is fathoms below us and there at its mouth are ships sailing in, rank upon rank of them, and they're innumerable, an armada blackening the sea and the great void below is pulling at me as I say, "So many—I never thought the sea had held so many," but Daedalus only points into a mirror's silver concavity which holds a light so bright it blinds me, for it's suddenly noon, and the mirrors blaze like a rank of suns, and their light is a bridge plunging down through the gulf of air to the prow of the foremost ship which kindles before my eyes, the orange flame engulfing its sails, and the wind brings faint screams and woodsmoke, as ship by ship the armada ignites, its rigid formations dissolving into an incandescent scrawl, and I know I should be rejoicing but my mind is full of angles of incidence and reflection, flash points, burn rates, luminosity.

When I reach Athens I present myself as a free-lance at its gate, though I'm ill-at-ease, for Theseus hates me and has many soldiers and my armies are far away. The slouching guard rubs his stubble and waves me through with hardly a glance and I master the impulse to call him to attention and say that I'm Minos, by god, whose hands are steeped in Athenian blood, and I demand the respect and the hatred that are due me, but in fact I say nothing and enter the city as no one in particular.

I've known Athens from a distance as an abstract locus of shipyards, fortification and supply, and I'm bemused to find myself wandering through the tangled streets, past the jumbled tombs, the walled gardens, the derelict factories, and the city seems to have a significance I can't quite name.

In the evenings I linger in the inns and the caravanserais nursing endless cups of watered wine and though I buy many drinks and listen carefully I hear of no new engineer in Theseus' court, no resurgent barbarian princes, no sage unraveling the riddles of antiquity. An officious Theban mercenary says he knows a Cretan when he hears one and wants to know what I'm doing in Attica; I tell him I've come to find a certain teacher of mathematics, and when he asks the teacher's name I have to overcome an absurd reluctance to say it's Daedalus, Daedalus who I'm seeking.

One day in the agora I find walls covered with graf-

fiti and among the lovers' names and vulgar drawings
is a row of scribbled symbols that seem almost to float
off of the wall, that seem almost to glow, and I realize
that what I'd taken at first for a haphazard scrawl is in
fact a theorem of the first water, and at first I'm rapt
and then relieved for Daedalus' style is unmistakable.

A few feet away are men with serious faces and
chalk on their hands, deep in conversation. I say,
"Where is the man who wrote that on the wall?"

"That?" says one. "That's nothing, just some
rubbish—it's been there for months."

"Who wrote it," I ask again, controlling my breathing, and again he says he doesn't know and turns away
from me, and I'm relieved to finally have a tangible
enemy. I tap him on the shoulder and when he turns
I punch him in the face, and when he clutches his
nose I drive my knee into his stomach. "*Who wrote
it*," I ask again as I draw my sword and he raises his
hand to ward off the blow that doesn't come for in his
terror there's an innocence that gives me pause, and
then he and the other men have scattered and someone's shouting for the guard. If I'm to meet Theseus
again I don't care to do it in chains so I scramble over
a wall and run through a maze of alleys and soon find
the gates and leave Athens behind.

Daedalus is the father of weapons and I expect to find
war in the wastes between cities but in the event there
are no crumbled walls, no shattered towns, no siege

trains sprawled across the desert, just city walls rising where I'd looked to find ruins.

Before the walls of Thebes I find an old man drawing diagrams in the sand and mumbling about geometry. He has dried gruel in his beard and can't bear to look me in the eye but his work has a grace and fluency I think I recognize. Having learned discretion I spend weeks listening to him ramble on about his work before I dare to drop a hint that I, too, have known a great teacher, one he might know himself, but he ignores me, even when I repeat myself, and then something breaks in me and I seize his shoulder and insist that he tell me how and when he knew Daedalus but he writhes weakly in my grasp and weeps with fear and there's nothing for it but to swallow my rage, let him go and move on.

I'm sleeping rough in the hills on the road to Arcadia on a night of brilliant cold clarity and wake with the full moon in my eyes and before the fog of sleep disperses I realize I know what the moon's phase was a year ago, and a century ago, and what it will be in ten thousand years, but how I know this is closed to me.

One day in Corinth I'm hungry and find all my gold spent. I could turn mercenary, but that's beneath the dignity of a king and of no interest to a mathematician, so I trade my sword for bread. It gives me pause to be without a weapon but I'm no longer afraid of being recognized and in fact am often mistaken for a holy man or scholar.

Soon it seems I've always been walking through the white dust of Attica. Sometimes I wonder what will become of me, a line of thought that raises questions that can only be avoided by stopping and reading the book. In each new city I seek out the mathematicians, who often seem to be expecting me and are generally kind, though I always find them disappointing; I'd been expecting men of my friend's caliber but almost invariably their technique is crude even by my standards. When they ask me to critique their work I do so honestly, which is to say I tell them it's worthless, except in those rare cases when it has a beauty in which I recognize my friend's hand. When I confront them they insist on pretending that Daedalus is a figure out of parable, or perhaps a way of speaking, and it's shocking how much this wounds me. My despair deepens as my acuity grows and I find his imprimatur in the faded graffiti on temple walls, in patterns of white stones scattered by road, in the striations of dust storms, in the sickly illumination of thunderheads, and I wonder who it was who once served me.

I sometimes hear that Daedalus has been seen in this city or that but as much as I pursue I never can find him, and I wonder why he still flees from me, as he must know by now that my anger is gone, that I just want to see him again, even for a few minutes, and talk about the book.

In one city in the endless succession of cities someone says, "But are you not him?"

"Not who?" I say.

"Daedalus," he says, smiling, looking intently into my face, and I laugh and admit that though once I was his master now I've lost him.

I'm sitting in the sun in a garden colonnade in what I think is Athens and my host, whose work verges on the competent, dips his bread in olive oil as he says, "We're founding an academy, my friends and I, to which we hope to attract the best minds." I nod abstractedly and he waits a beat and then says, "We'd be honored, of course, if you'd join us." I'm taken by surprise, but there's something to be said for an end to wandering, and a garden of my own where I could sit and think through ancient problems away from the road's dust and weariness, and perhaps there'd even be a woman, and for a moment I think of going back to Crete—I'm king, so why not?—but the pomp and intrigue belong to someone else's life. That night asleep in the guest room the book's logic burns behind my eyes and I wake certain that the academy is a trap and steal silently out into the garden and then over the wall into the night.

Soon I'm in high broken country where there's no

road and in that solitude my mind becomes a void the book rushes in to fill. I find a shallow cave in an arroyo scoured by the wind and as the day passes nothing moves but the light and the shadow gliding over the stone. I read while the light lasts and my thoughts crystallize around the negative space of the blank pages at the book's end. Somehow I know Daedalus isn't far away, and is coming ever closer, and if he ever arrives I'll embrace him, tell him all is forgiven, and show him that I, even I, have attained a certain standard of mathematics.

Time passes, and sometimes I find bread and water waiting at the cave-mouth, which I accept without question. I have the book by heart now—in fact, I know it so well I feel I wrote it. I'm surprised to find a few mistakes, but it seems even Daedalus erred, that even he was getting old. I have an intuition of how the book would have ended had Daedalus had time to finish, and had he still been the man he once was, but though I try a long time it won't quite come into focus. I wish I were more intelligent and am on the verge of giving up but instead I accept that the failure and the pain will always be with me forever and shortly thereafter I know how to end the book.

I write out the last pages, and as the ink dries I know I'm alone, and that Daedalus has been dead a long time. I wonder how I'd ever been content to be no more than a king and a soldier, blind to all the beauty in the world.

With the book finished, I feel absolutely empty. I

hear a raven's rattling croak and a wind in the arroyo but otherwise the world is still. I wonder if I'll die soon, and if it matters. I know that Daedalus himself couldn't have done better, but I'm without vanity, for names and persons are ephemeral—in the end, there's only pattern.

21

DAEDALUS

Daedalus worked as an engineer but was foremost a pure mathematician.

Exhorting a crowd of faceless students, Daedalus says, "Number is the language and the substance of the world, and its sole certainty." But then a student—the brightest, and the most nearly individuated of the lot—steps forward and says, *"But teacher, what then is the length of this line in the sand?"*

Daedalus, who has the gift of knowing measure at a glance, looks down at the curved line drawn in the sand at his feet and starts to speak, but as the first numbers pass his lips he sees that his answer is inexact, and adds a digit to amend it, but even then an error remains, so he adds another, and though the error dwindles it doesn't disappear even after the tenth, the thousandth, the ten thousandth revision; the line seems to rush toward him, and with great clarity he sees the scarred prismatic mountains of the sand grains as the digits surge by.*

He struggles, at first, as the number pours over him, and is distantly aware of the passing of the millionth and then the billionth digits, and still the progression roars on. As the initial panic subsides he reflects that the torrent of random numbers is as meaningless and as comforting as rain pattering on a rooftop, and the digits flow past unremarked, and his thoughts become a grey blur as his old life comes to seem remote, like a ghost hastening off into evening.

Numbers, he recalls, can correspond to letters, and now in the flood of digits he finds words, and these multiply and coalesce into sentences, and then paragraphs and then whole books (all of which are extraordinary rarities, tiny islands punctuating the seas of white noise which he has perforce learned to ignore). The first books are contemptible—so much ineptly edited hackwork—but soon there are reasonable volumes, and to his surprise, he finds his own books among them, both those he has written and those he has planned—with apprehension and delight he recognizes his own unmistakable voice in a treatise on number theory he has consistently neglected to write.

The digits' flow is unabating, and whole libraries wash by. Some of the books are about him, chastising

---

*The mathematicians of antiquity were familiar with irrational numbers—π, for instance—whose digits wind on forever without pattern or repetition.

his hubris, praising his resilience, or telling the story of his incarceration in a number as both a parable and a dream.

The books grow in complexity, and gradually become simulacra of the world. At first they're no more than caricatures—atlases drawn in crude lines, vague islands implied with shadow—but soon (not soon as he once measured time, but, of necessity, he has learned patience) there are cities of a certain verisimilitude and then he reads that he is walking through the cool shadow of the stone arcades on his way to the courtyard where the faceless students sit waiting. He takes his place before them and draws breath to resume his polemic as though he had never been interrupted.

"*You have beheld the number,*" says the brightest student, who is terrible now.

"I've seen a finite sequence of digits, no more and no less," he replies.

"*Must you see more?*" asks the student, possibly with regret.

"It would be to no purpose—there could only be more of the same. Either there is no number, or I have always been in the number," says Daedalus, and continues.

22

PHILEMON
AND BAUCIS

*Zeus came to town disguised as a traveler. He went
from door to door but only Philemon and Baucis were
hospitable. Zeus destroyed the town but rewarded the
couple.*

The rain clatters on the roof as the stranger drinks his
wine and smiles at the boy and girl across the table.
"You took me in, when no one else would," he says,
"so I'll give you the gift of whatever you choose." Under
the table the boy's fingers twine around the girl's; the
stranger is motionless, his eyes fixed on them; far away
the river roars, and the boy has the sense their guest
will sit there waiting forever, if necessary, but he wills
himself to speak and says, "We want to stay together,"
at which the girl nods.

"It's granted," says the stranger, "and gladly, for
tonight there is death enough."

"Who are you, sir?" asks the boy, but the stranger
rises, kisses them both, and goes out the door. They

look for him from their threshold but there's only pouring rain, mud, the dark.

They hold each other through the night. The walls of their hut, reverberating in the wind, are a fragile barrier against the storm, but they have nowhere else to go. When dawn comes they find the sky clear and the forest shattered, the sodden hillsides collapsed, and the town down in the valley washed away. They climb down the now-trackless slopes with the idea of helping but find only granite boulders the size of cattle, smooth swathes of black mud where houses were, the fragments of temple pillars protruding from a silty pool.

They search the hills for days, unable to believe they're entirely alone, but find nothing living except a few stray sheep, which they bring home. There are broken beams and building stones in the river's new eddies, and over the course of weeks Philemon drags them up the hill and uses them to build a barn. The flood's silt makes good soil and their crops flourish where the village was though the first summer is lonely.

Their first child comes the year after the flood. Travelers come looking for the bones of their relatives but find nothing and leave after praying for the river to keep hold of its dead. Years pass, and brush grows thick and wild in the loess, and they have the land to themselves.

In the tenth year after the flood the summer is dry and the winter so bitter that the wolves come down from the mountains. One freezing day Philemon is drowsing by his flocks in a snow-covered meadow with bow in hand when he looks up to see half-starved men emerging from the wood, their spear-points gleaming, either escaped slaves or deserting soldiers but certainly desperate, and most likely a death sentence, for they've already seen him and are coming straight on. He draws a deep breath and shouts that raiders have come, and to send armed men, hoping the bandits will think he has friends and that his wife will escape with the children.

In the evening his eldest son slips out of the cave where his mother hid them; he has a sling, a pouch full of damp clay, and is too young to think death can touch him. He finds his father sitting on a stone watching ravens squabble over the bandits' corpses. Philemon says, "I shot at two, missed, and then they were on me and I'd lost the chance to run. They tried to kill me, and I expected to die, but as in a dream their weapons wouldn't bite, and I kept thinking it was a mistake I was still breathing. Finally I seized someone's sword and stabbed him in the neck, and then I killed the rest of them, one after another. The last two lost heart, and made signs against the evil eye as they tried to scramble off, but I caught up with them and they're dead too. One of them stabbed me with a spear when my back was turned, and hit so hard the haft broke—it tore my shirt, but didn't leave a bruise." His son helps him dig graves for the dead men, lest their ghosts haunt the mountain, and come summer they plant wheat between the mounds.

In the sixteenth year after the flood their eldest son goes away in spring and comes back in autumn with a wife who thinks at first her husband's parents are his siblings. The rest of the children marry and build homesteads in the valley and it isn't long before the first grandchild comes, but Philemon and Baucis don't change, and their family never speaks of it to strangers. When their eldest son dies they put him in the ground not far from the bandits' graves and when they're done weeping and their children have gone back to their houses Philemon says he's going away.

"Away," says Baucis. "What's away? Your family is here, and their families, and our valley—this is your place."

"There are other valleys, other cities," he says. "How can I say I've lived? I've never stood in the line of battle. I have never beheld the sea."

"You've known love, and death, and terror—you've even spoken with the gods," she says. "Everything that is, is here. And what is here, is elsewhere, but for me."

He says, "I'll be back," kisses her cheek, and walks off into the hills without looking back.

When he finally returns he's lean, hungry and worn. His great-grandson, who's standing guard on the valley road, would have sent him away but his great-grandmother, the matriarch, has taught him to be hospitable. Philemon finds Baucis in their old house, which has grown new wings since he last saw it, though she hasn't changed at all. She says, "What did you find in the world?"

"Men with hearts and spears of bronze running to die under a rain of black arrows," he says. "Ships breasting white seas. White cities full of secrets. A shrine where the god spoke in the whisper of oak-leaves. An island fortress where mirrors glitter on the battlements and set fire to ships with their concentrated light. I have killed in righteousness, and in anger, and held a hero's head on my lap while he died. I've won gold, more than we once could've dreamt of, and lost it all."

"And now?" asks Baucis.

"And now," he says, "I'm back."

She tells him who's married, given birth, and moved away, and how everyone in town calls her Grandmother. She's a midwife, her face the first her descendants see and often the last as she nurses them through their agonies. She's grateful for long life because those she loves need never know the world without her.

Philemon and the young men go down to the valley floor and exhume the stones of the old drowned village which they use to build a wall around their town and a temple to Zeus the Traveler. Baucis plants an orchard within the wall and by the time the town over-spills its walls she's harvesting its apples.

"All these children," she says one night as they lie in their old bed. "Consumed by their desires, by all their little loves and hates. Could anyone ever have been so young? I look at them and feel unnecessary."

"Then let us go away," he says.

"When?"

"Now." He writes a note for their eldest surviving grandson, and they slip off into the night.

They're gone for years and when they finally come back the town has become a city of marble temples, tall houses, soldiers in burnished helms. The field where he buried the raiders has become farmland, the mounds barely detectable. They see echoes of their own faces in the city's aristocracy but now there are foreigners and slaves and strangers, and when by secret signs they make themselves known to the city's lord he looks at them quizzically, then laughs and embraces them, says he saw them when he was a boy but never thought they'd be back, had never really believed his grandfather's stories, but for all that he welcomes them, and says he'll gladly cede his throne. Their fingers entwined, they say no, it isn't necessary.

In a certain valley there's a city of white towers and banners shivering in the wind that's said to be haunted by demons who watch and keep it and have the likeness of a boy and girl. They look like any mortals and can only be recognized by their antiquated speech and their stillness.

They come and go; they live in distant kingdoms, take other lovers, part for years at a time. One day in Babylon Philemon is passing through the money-lenders' quarter and sees Baucis washing baby clothes in a fountain. He greets her gallantly and courts her through that city's luminous summer nights and soon he abandons his troop of mercenaries and she her most recent husband; when they come home over seas and high mountains they find their city burned, the walls crumbled, the valley abandoned, its fields sewn with salt. They rebuild their house in the same place it stood before, and more children come, and a new town rises, and they go away and come back again, and one night on an empty road they decide it's been enough.

They go to the temple of Zeus the Traveler and find their old guest waiting. "We're done," they say, "and ready for the end," but their guest shakes his head and says, "Death separates, and I promised that you'd never be apart."

Baucis says, "Is there no escape, then? Are we prisoners of the world?" but he smiles at them and kisses them both once, and later the citizens find two trees growing in the temple courtyard, their trunks twined together, and their leaves neither faded nor fell as generations slept in their shade, their branches thickened, and their roots reached deeper.

PART IV

NEMESIS

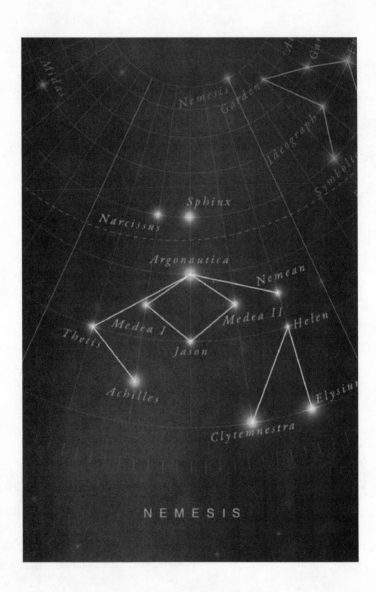

NARCISSUS

Narcissus was the most beautiful of men. Tiresias warned him to fear mirrors. Nemesis undid him.

Beautiful rooms full of light and fire and everyone pretending not to look at me. I was much desired, by rich boys with their hearts breathily on their sleeves, rich mens' wives *d'un certain âge* in a lot of kohl, urbane and athletic Athenians who spoke of friendship and excellence, spend-thrifty wine-factors whose chins trembled when I breathed on them. They offered gifts, which I accepted, and verses, which were always the same—I was perfect, moving and unmoved and flawless as stone, and the like. I never let them touch me, but gave them every chance to sigh.

I'd been in Sybaris forever, it seemed, sleeping through the days and passing the nights in an endless succession of identical parties that left no more lasting impression than reflected voices, repeated conversations, wine-fumes and claustrophobia. I had friends or, rather, people I drank with, all of whom found inexhaustible delight in the company of louche musicians, noblemen in thin disguise, fire-dancers, fire-eaters, slaves with interesting histories, the more articulate sort of whore. In the false dawn, on the way home, when the wine was fading, I knew it was perilous to stay too long, that the demimonde must have a term, that it was, in fact, a banal and mediocre bohemia, but it was home, if home was anywhere, and when I tried to focus on another future my mind wandered.

One night at a party someone quenched all the torches and left us fumbling in the dark, which delighted most of the celebrants, judging by the whispers and the laughter. Unseen strangers groped me and moved on; I'd never liked to be touched, and was searching for a place out of the flow when a hand closed on my wrist. The fingers were calloused and the ragged, broken nails dug into my skin. "Who is it?" I asked, and tried to pull away, but whoever it was was strong and I found I could smell him, his sweat and unwashed clothes and something metallic. Behind us a bonfire roared into life and I found myself looking into the face of an old man, a stranger, scars where his eyes had been. He said, "Narcissus, loveliest of men, fear mirrors." I was going to ask him why, for I'd seen mirrors and been none the worse for it (though privately I thought my reputation for beauty was exaggerated) but there was a shriek of laughter behind me and I turned to see a girl standing by the fire with a clique of notably bitchy actors. She was dressed like they were, and stood like them, so much the thespian that I thought at first she must be a boy in drag, but no, there were breasts, or the beginnings of them—she was about thirteen. She stood between Thyestes the tragedian, who had a patronizing arm around her shoulders, and Bagoas, nobleman and occasional libertine, who was making a show of looking out into the crowd though all his attention was on the girl. Thyestes made most of his money off the stage. She doesn't know what's going to happen, I thought. She caught my eye and smiled, almost convulsively; I nodded to her and turned away but the blind man was already lost in the press of bodies and instead I found Artabazos, nominal playwright, gossip extraordinaire. "Who's the little thing with the actors?" I asked.

"Ah, the ingenue? Echo is her name. Echo from the provinces. Echo had a lover—her first, you see—rich family, vehement objections, but they had plenty of daughters, and it was easier to let her go. He dropped her, of course, and she washed up here. Thyestes found her sitting in an alley, filthy and sodden, hands folded in her lap, staring straight ahead; at first she wouldn't speak, then insisted she was nothing, no one and nameless, but now, as you can see, she's very much at home."

He paused, emotion moving over his face like weather. "Come home and have a drink with me, my dear. I have more to tell you," he said, standing too close, vinous and flushing.

"My excellent friend, I'm afraid I *can't* go home

with you—the truth is I don't like you very much and you're too poor to be worth deceiving." Someone next to me laughed wheezily—I was regarded as a wit on the basis of such remarks, though they were only the truth.

The party faded as parties will and it was too hot and too dark in the many low rooms so I decided to go home, but while I was looking for an exit I found myself on a balcony where Bagoas held the girl, Echo, in a sprawling embrace. I would have left them but I saw the rigor in her face, how she clutched her arms to her chest, how her shirt was half torn away.

If I have a principle it's that tricks should be treated genteelly. I said, "Bagoas, you're a pompous and mediocre nobody. No one likes you very much and you're welcome only when you're paying, though you seem not, till now, to have known it. Also, I hear you're often impotent, so why don't you leave the girl and go practice raping your horses, or better yet your dogs?" Such spectacular rudeness can overwhelm the unprepared but Bagoas, to his credit, I suppose, glared at me, fumbled for his dagger and stood. I should have been afraid but I wasn't, as in fact I was never afraid, though I couldn't have said why—I've never been a warrior. I put on the expressionless mask I wore when I wanted to drop an admirer and said, "The captain of the praetorian said he'd do anything for a smile from me. What do you think he'd do to you if I gave him a kiss? I'm thinking something with hot iron and a saw." I smiled pleasantly and watched his face, wondering what would happen next. He gave me a look intended to convey that this wasn't over, that one day he would find me and et cetera, and stalked away.

Echo had neither moved nor blinked. I arranged the remnants of her shirt over her frightfully skinny shoulders and said, "These people. No manners. Very disagreeable."

"These people," she said, in a voice radiant with detachment and inflected with contempt and just a little mirth that, after a moment, I recognized as a fair imitation of my own. "No manners. Very disagreeable." I laughed and asked if she'd been hurt, by which I meant raped, but she only looked at me wide-eyed, her need almost palpable, so I stood, murmured what was no doubt good advice, and left.

There were other stations in the night but when the sky was lightening I finally went home. I lived on a posh, tree-lined avenue where drunks and vagrants were relatively rare so I was surprised to see someone curled up on my doorstep, apparently asleep, sucking her thumb—it was the girl. I prodded her with my toe and said, "You. Wake up." She opened her eyes and I said, "I'm no one's gallant, and I'm not running an orphanage, or a brothel, so go home, or, as the case may be, away." She blinked back tears, and then, in the haughty, weary drawl of an empress addressing a pauper she advised me to go practice raping my horses, or, better yet, my dogs.

I said, "I have neither horses nor dogs, my dear, so it will have to be *you*," and squinted at her with such carnal menace as I could muster. She looked up at me, wide-eyed, considering, and I was about to say something else when she launched herself at me, locking her arms around my waist, her fragile warmth pressing into me, and though I recoiled—I don't like to be touched, and even my most munificent admirers buy themselves only a prolonged agony—she wouldn't drop the embrace, despite my exasperated sighs and ostentatious throat-clearing, and finally I returned it.

My house was large but I only used two rooms so she had her pick of empty ones. I had almost no furniture so I made her a bed from a pile of my furs and told her she'd sleep like a Scythian princess. I sent the maid out for food, which Echo ate with distressing avidity, and for wine, which I watered when she wasn't looking, in which she matched me cup for cup. I asked her about herself, where she was from, who her parents were and what had happened with Thyestes, but she only smiled at me and wouldn't say a word.

It was good to have a pet. She'd be sprawled on pillows in the foyer when I came home from an assignation. I'd show her the haul from that night's admirer and we'd rate it for taste and extravagance. I let her decide how nice I'd be the next time I saw them. And we talked, or rather I talked, though I wasn't naturally loquacious, but she encouraged me, and somehow I told her everything I knew.

I had my tailor cut my old clothes to fit her. I put jewels on her ear-lobes and on her wrists and on her clavicles. She wasn't beautiful, but her face was broad and blank, all strong planes and shadows; she was an empty canvas for my brush, and I painted her face as I painted my own. We looked like twins, when I was done, or lovers, or both. We were lovely.

When we went out all eyes were on us. Everyone wondered if I'd finally taken a lover, which was good for business as it gave the marks hope. She was a great social asset, chattering tirelessly when I was stupefied with boredom, and if her opinions were second-hand she'd overheard a great many and delivered them all with brio and conviction. We finished each other's sentences, and ate from the same plate, and she draped herself around me. We made a point of snubbing Thyestes. I welcomed each night, and all the nights blurred together, and she was always close by. I thought those nights would never end, and somehow at the same time that we'd leave one day and live together, far away, in a quiet house by a river, and never come back to the city.

Some governor's son paid court to her, which I tolerated, though I insisted that she stay intact, for I wanted neither a screaming infant nor a spotty aristocrat in the household. When he became importunate I told her to drop him but she said she didn't know how. "There's nothing to it," I said. "Just look into his eyes and say . . . nothing. *What's wrong?* he'll ask. *Are you angry?* He'll apologize for imaginary slights, for stinginess, for other lovers. *Do you hate me?* he'll ask. *Have I taught you to despise me?* Why *won't you talk to me?* His sad mouth will tremble, and if he's not really a gentleman there may be harsh words and tears, and then it's over."

Nemesis was a frightful goddess whose name was rarely spoken and the good burghers of Sybaris would have been shocked to learn that there was a party in her temple, which was, I supposed, the point of being there. The place made me uncomfortable, all footsteps and shadows and never enough light. It was too dim to see faces but I recognized Rukshana, a minor royal, from her slouch. Rukshana liked a bit of rough, preferring beards and scars to smooth chins and clean lines; she had, to my certain knowledge, fucked her way through the entire praetorian. We were chummy. It was a long way from her to a throne (though never far to a bar-stool) but she still had the High Palace manner and their breathy, lisping drawl.

"Slumming, dear?" I asked.

"Oh, no," said Rukshana, "these are quite my people. Salt of the earth, and so on. Who's your little friend?" Echo, lately of an alley, lifted up her hand to be kissed.

I'd never been in that temple before and as they talked my eyes drifted up to a statue of Nemesis, larger than life, and her face wasn't what I expected, full of wild pride and terror and desperation, and when I looked back Echo and Rukshana were gone. I searched for them throughout the temple but found only strangers.

I'd thought she'd be waiting at home but when I got there the house was empty. I waited up for her, supposing she'd left the party to find her lover, but dawn came and she still wasn't there and finally I fell asleep on her pillows.

I woke in the evening but she still hadn't come back so I went out looking, though I found nothing that night or the next night or the next, and I hardly slept, and I kept thinking I saw her and being disappointed, and finally at some nobleman's fête I found Artabazos drunk on a divan and he said he hadn't seen Echo but he had seen Rukshana, who had a new friend, a protégée, who was little more than a girl. "And it wasn't Echo?" I said.

"No, it wasn't your guttersnipe. I haven't found out her name, yet, but she was clearly of one of the great houses of Persia, not at all your kind."

I flirted my way into the palace and waited motionless in the shadows of the orangery near Rukshana's rooms, watching the courtiers come and go, and when Echo finally walked by in her aristocrat's disguise I hardly recognized her.

"Echo!" I called, sick with relief, but she didn't slow, and I ran after her and put my hand on her shoulder. "You might have told me you were going to be away. I know how it is, obviously, so go have your run, but then come home." I smiled at her but she stared at me without expression. "Oh, I see," I said, "your new connection with a third-rate demi-royal has put you above speaking. Don't let me detain you—by all means return to your proper palace, or was it an alley?" Her face was motionless, her eyes cold. "Have I offended you? Neglected you? Is there *anything* I haven't done for you? Look. Have your prince, or your princess, or all the royals in a row for all I care, but then come back, because it's us against everyone, and we'll take what they have and give them nothing in return and love only each other, so come home. Echo?" I said, but she was already walking away, and I realized I'd been wrong, that she'd always been beautiful.

I looked for her a long time. They barred me from the palace but it didn't matter because from what I heard she didn't last there long. I went to parties high and low, sifted every dive, flop-house and brothel, every place where the discarded might wash up, but she was never there, and I rarely slept, and drank too much, and ate too much poppy. My new round must have been hard on me because old acquaintances looked startled when they saw me and I finally took the seer's advice and stayed away from mirrors. I started waking up in places I didn't know, and the recent past was riddled with dark stretches, and one day it was winter and I was looking for her by the freezing river outside the city walls and it had been a long time since I'd eaten, and though it was a bright, frigid day when I closed my eyes it was twilight when I opened them, and there was another river before me, this one swift and black and smooth as glass. I peered into the flow and my heart lifted when I thought I saw her looking up at me.

24

SPHINX

The sphinx was the daughter of Nemesis. Monster and oracle, she was her supplicants' ruin. She lived in the desert near Thebes.

Oedipus was the great-great-grandson of Cadmus, Thebes' founder.

In the last light the desert sand and the sphinx were all but indistinguishable as she said, "All that is, is written here." At her feet lay worn planes of fractured granite, incised with minute writing that Oedipus stooped to trace with the fingers of one hand while the other held his spear leveled at her heart. Finally, he lowered his eyes and read:

> Oedipus crept over the desert through the evening dimness, fragments of ancient bone crumbling under his feet, but he didn't see the sphinx until she was right before him. A sense of rising grace and mass like waves cresting and then

she was settling on her haunches, intent on him, as he brought his spear to bear. "They say the sphinx is first among oracles," he said, "and that where others see shadows she sees all. They say she's always hungry, but always speaks the truth."

She said, "The world is a book I know by heart, and its verses the substance of my days and my dreaming."

"At Delphi they told me I'm doomed to turn patricide and worse, so I'm here to learn how to shape the future."

In the last light the desert sand and the sphinx were all but indistinguishable as she said, "All that is, is written here." At her feet lay worn planes of fractured granite, incised with minute writing that Oedipus stooped to trace with the fingers of one hand while the other held his spear leveled at her heart. Finally, he lowered his eyes and read.

He heard the sand creak as her weight shifted at which he looked up and threw his spear through her heart.

He heard the sand creak as her weight shifted at which he slipped off to one side, scanning the gloom, spear raised to kill her, but the lunge he expected didn't come. He stood there peering into the shadows and then felt her hot breath on his neck.

He propped his spear on the sand, sighed, and

waited to die. "I never threw my spear," he said. "Therefore, your book is false. There's that, at least."

"You never cast your spear," she agreed as she twined her arms around his chest and pulled him into an iron embrace. "But the book is true. Therefore, we are not in the book."

"But if the book is the world, where then are we?"

"Someplace else. In an undreamed dream, a tale unwritten."

"To what possible end?" he asked, voice finally cracking.

She rubbed her smooth cheek against his, redolent of musk and blood. "Perhaps I knew you'd come to kill me, and have always been waiting. Perhaps I've loved you a long time, and never wanted you to know."

"So what now?"

"The rest," she said, "is like a blank page."

25

ARGONAUTICA

Jason was prince of Iolcos and the first cousin of Alcestis. He went to sea with his Argonauts in search of the Golden Fleece of Colchis.

The day was windless and sweltering but the *Argo*'s oars rose and dipped and rose again. Jason had called a contest to see who was strongest, and the crew's arms and backs burned, but still they strained, telling themselves they were heroes of high lineage and too proud to fail, but as the hours passed they faltered one by one. They were heading toward a steep island when Peleus dropped his oar and Herakles pulled on alone, as relentless as the waves, until one of his oars snapped and he was left sweating and staring at its stump as the *Argo* coasted on.

They'd known his reputation when the *Argo* sailed, how his rage melted men like snow in hot sun. They'd offered him the captaincy, but he'd declined in Jason's favor; this would have been exquisite humility in

another man but Herakles had a habit of looking
out to sea while Jason was talking, waiting for him
to finish, or nearly, so he could do what needed to be
done.

They threw themselves down on the sand. The island was abandoned; no path led up among the blue
pines on the mountain. The day was ending, and their
thoughts turned to a fire, and how such fires were like
jewels when seen at night from the sea, when Jason
said they'd build an altar to Nemesis, who was said to
dwell in those parts. The men rose groaning to gather
stones but Herakles, who'd been at a distance, saw
what they were doing and heaved up a sea-boulder half
as large as a house, the salt water pouring through
his beard and hair as he carried it to the beach, set it
down and said, "There's your altar," and went off up
the mountain to cut a new oar.

Peleus threw his stone into the surf and said, "We're
nothing next to him. Our enemies might as well make
war on the sun. We're little men to fill out the ship's
company."

As the evening settled the wind rose, sending
shivers through the pines and raising the surf, and the
Argo groaned on the beach, each receding wave pulling it back toward the water, and in silence the men
did the rest. No orders were given as they sheeted the
sail, and no one looked back as the wind bore them
away, so no one saw the garnet spark of the fire high
on the mountain's slope. Herakles sat beside it, chin on
hand, watching them go.

26

NEMEAN

Herakles was the son of Zeus, bound to serve his half-brother Eurystheus, the king of Thebes. One of his labors was the destruction of the Nemean lion, an ancient monster whose hide was impervious to weapons. Herakles later killed his children in a fit of madness.

Herakles was hiding in the trees when the first light touched the water. A gazelle emerged from tall grass and blue shadow, sniffed the air and bent to drink. Explosive motion, a flash of gold, grasses waving wildly and then a flock of birds gabbling into the air as he heard the crack of thick bone breaking.

The lion came up the trail with the gazelle dangling from its mouth—it was huge, like something in a dream. If it was ancient, it showed no sign of it, its golden flanks scarless.

Herakles stepped out of the trees and fired an arrow at its heart. He was already nocking his second arrow when the first ricocheted off the lion's breast, and then it was like it was falling at him, and there was just time to pick up his club.

As the lion leapt he swung at its skull but when the blow landed his hands seemed to shatter and the club went spinning off into the air. The lion's momentum almost knocked him down, which would have been the end, but he kept his feet as it pushed him back through the dust. Drowning in its strength, its claws impaling his shoulders, he made an absolute effort but it was like trying to throw a mountain. He'd never been over-matched before, and it must have felt his dismay because it pressed him harder and over-committed its weight. "There's my life back," he thought gratefully, for no seasoned wrestler would have made that mistake; he yielded a step, opening space into which the lion stumbled, then stepped in, wrapped an arm around its neck and squeezed.

Its claws scrabbled at him, trying to find purchase, opening furrows in his back, but he fixed his eyes on the sky and tightened his choke-hold, ignoring what was happening to the rest of his body. (There's no pain, he told himself, and it's rain running down my back.) As the lion's wind ebbed its struggles weakened, and their clinch became an embrace, and finally he laid its dead weight down.

He slumped to the ground, resting against the body, his mind wandering as his blood ran in rivulets around his legs. He was shivering, though the day was hot; his camp, a mile away through the woods, seemed unattainable. The hide, he thought, but his dagger snapped on the golden skin without leaving a mark. His vision greyed, cleared, greyed again as he hefted the lion's fore-paw, extruded a hooked claw and opened an incision in its belly. The flies came as he degloved its rear legs. The flayed hide was thick and heavy, still warm with life's heat; he wrapped himself up in it, ignoring the bloody integument, and fell asleep.

He woke to see the lion's raw musculature gleaming purple in the twilight, crows and jackdaws chattering in the trees. Freezing where the air touched him, he pulled the hide closer.

When next he woke the carcass was black and desiccated. He worried that wolves would come, but of course the hide was impenetrable. The lion's jaws framed a square of waving boughs where he thought someone was watching him, and he wondered if it was Hermes, come to tell him his time was over and his service done. He twisted in the hide to shut out the dusk.

In the night he heard rasping breath like rolling surf. *I was never supposed to die*, said the lion. Herakles shook his head to clear it and went back to sleep.

In the morning it spoke to him again. *Nothing could touch me—no blade, no fang, not even time*, it said. *I would have lived forever. I would have seen the world through. By what right did you extinguish my life?* He tried in vain to find the energy to argue as it said, *You, whose only virtue is strength, whose soul is nothing but hunger and a fathomless, inarticulate rage. You, who were born to be the slave of the intelligent.*

He wept, for he knew it was true—it was why the Argonauts had abandoned him—and said, "Why are you still here? You're dead, and there's an end. Go to Hell and let me be."

It said, *I was the last relict of old night, and now I'm gone. The world is poorer for your having been in it.*

The next morning he was strong enough to stand, though his back was reticulated with ridged scars, red and puffy with infection. The carcass had turned to blackened leather, yellow vertebrae erupting through the shrinking flesh. The lion's skin clung to him like fitted armor, and its jaws were a sort of helmet. When he washed in the lake, the lion looked up at him from the water.

His eyes kept closing on the road back to Thebes but when he stumbled the lion was there to guide him. It told him stories of past ages when it stalked animals the size of siege-engines over vast plains and life had been joy and blood and strife unending. Snapping out of his doze, Herakles found himself standing before Eurystheus, who was haranguing him, red-faced, spittle flying, and he didn't know what to say, but then the lion was whispering in his ear. It was articulate—clever, even—far more than he'd ever been, and as he wasn't needed he drifted away.

He dreamed of the hunt. Now and then he woke up, once finding himself firing arrows into a cloud of

bronze birds wheeling in the sky, and once to find himself standing before an advancing army, and when he
looked back he saw his own soldiers waiting for the
signal to charge. The last time, he found himself in his
children's rooms, though the children weren't there,
and there was blood on his hands and on the walls and
the ceiling. (Somewhere there was a dull thrum like
distant purring.) At first he was alarmed, but then realized he'd been wrong, that what he'd thought was his
house was in fact a pier of low rock protruding from
the plain, that the blood on his hands was from three
young baboons, torn apart by some predator. Relieved,
he dismissed Thebes from his mind and set out across
the plain, full of joy, keen for the chase, looking for
spoor in the sighing grasses.

27

MEDEA I

Medea was a witch and a princess of Colchis. Jason wanted her to help him get the Golden Fleece, which was guarded by Ladon, an immortal serpent.

In the mountains at the end of the world you finally come to the valley of the fleece. It's redolent of moss and stone, and water drips contrapuntally into shallow pools from high seeps. Raptors float on thermals, passing from the sunlight into the shadows of the cliffs, but there's no sign of other animals, not even tracks in the sand. A weathered sign in the hand-writing of another age is nailed to a tree—*beyond me*, it says, *death waits*. Your father told you there's a serpent in the glade, bound there by the gods in ancient days, endlessly wise, always watching, full of hate.

The serpent must be long gone, you think, but as you pass the sign the bird-song stops and the wind brings dry rot and metal and there's a sudden sense of breathless intensity. You freeze, sifting the world's murmur for signs, but hear nothing. Your nerve breaks and you're turning to go when you see me coiled in the branches.

You don't flinch, and that's why I listen rather than strike. In a strong clear voice you tell me that Jason, your new lover, wants you to get the fleece and then sail away with him leaving Colchis forever. Your father says Jason is an adventurer of obscure family and suspect intent, and would mistreat you as soon as he could get away with it. Who should you believe?

My malice has been blunted by the torpor of centuries but now I need only speak the plain truth, which is that your father cares for nothing but his kingdom and regards you as his property, and that behind the lovely planes of Jason's face there's little but vanity, a need for approval and a restless, inarticulate ambition. He'll push you aside when another woman comes along and then resent you for being wounded. Knowing this, you'll go with him anyway.

28

MEDEA II

When he was little more than a boy Jason chanced to meet a demon named Medea, who made him the sole object of her desire and pursued him relentlessly as he fled across the seas. Catching him, she gave him no rest, being out of reach when he wanted her and breathing on him when, exhausted, he only wanted sleep. He cursed her vainly, though in the course of his misadventures she often saved his life, raising her little finger to still storms, stop hearts, sink ships.

Only when he'd resigned himself to suffering did she admit that she loved him, and long had, and promised to torment him no more. He demanded proof, so she said she would restore his aging father's youth. Distrusting her, Jason followed secretly when she led the old man into the wood, and saw her cut his throat and let the black blood pour out into a wooden tub. He sprang out of hiding and struck her with his sword but the blade wouldn't bite so he fled back to their house and sealed it against her. All night she sat outside what had been their door, howling to be let in, her despair shaking the city. When he proved unrelenting she started changing her shape, first into a serpent, then into a fire, and then into a wolf who tore their two children to bloody rags. Finally she became a storm that shattered windows and tore the surface of the sea, but the wind soon blew out and she was never heard from again.

29

JASON

Jason lived quietly after Medea killed his father and their children.

I found my father sitting on my doorstep. It was evening, and he'd been dead for years, and he was little more than a boy, but I recognized him at once, though it looked like he hadn't slept in days, and of course I thought I was dreaming. As a gesture toward common sense I told him to get up and go, as I had neither time nor coin for beggars, but his face crumpled and he said, *God damn you, god damn you anyway for leaving me out here in the dark*, so I let him in.

I watched him as he ate and couldn't bring myself to ask questions lest I break whatever tenuous spell had brought him back. It wasn't long before his eyes glazed, and his chin sank toward his chest; I said, "You have come a long way, and you are welcome here, but now it's time to rest."

I lit candles in my study and tried to read but the

words on the page were black marks without meaning so I went and stood in the door to his room, where I thought to find him vanished, or transformed, but there he was, eyes closed, sleeping.

He slept through the afternoon, and the light was fading when I found him sitting up in his room. He was shaking, as though he had a fever, and he said he was cold, so I propped him up in bed and covered him with blankets and listened as his mind wandered. I was relieved he was confused, and ashamed to be relieved, but I thought he might not ask about the children, and in fact he rambled on about hunts he'd known as a boy, how he'd plunged through thick forests that stretched down to the city walls, and of the sun, which had been brighter back then, when all the animals spoke, and of standing on the strand watching me board the *Argo*, and watching the *Argo* sail away.

When his eyes closed I seized his shoulder, suddenly convinced he'd not wake again, and my voice seemed faint and far away as I said, "But how have you come back? For you made that journey from which there's no returning."

He said, "There was pain, and blood, and bad dreams. I was thirsty, and I was looking for you, wandering in cities whose names I never knew, and no one understood me when I asked for help, and it was always cold, the cold unbelievable, and I thought I'd be lost forever, but then I found you," and then his eyes closed, and I watched him, as the hours passed, poised to rouse him if it seemed he would slip away, but he was only asleep, and before dawn I was asleep on the floor beside him.

I took him walking in the city. It was winter, and the streets were cased in ice, and the freezing fog made shadows of passersby. I lost him for a moment in the whiteness, and immediately I was certain he was gone forever, but then I heard a girl singing, and following her voice I found him before her, listening on a street-corner. I bought us hot wine; his hands were still clumsy, and spilled red drops stained the snow at our feet. He turned his face toward a momentary sun, and as his exhalations clouded and dispersed I wondered if every breath felt miraculous, and what he'd learned down there in the dark, but he said nothing through the short afternoon.

It was always evening then, and the harbor was frozen, and the city bound in snow, the snow falling endlessly as winter settled deeper. The fire burned low and we seemed always to have been in the shadows and flickering red heat of the low room by the garden. I wanted to ask what he planned to do with the new life before him, but it was easier to watch the snow fall beyond the window and the reflection of the dying fire that was the center of our night.

•

It wasn't long before it seemed like he'd been there forever and there was nothing more natural than keeping house with the dead. I kept no servants, first from poverty and then from discretion, and every day I rose early to mend the fire and make the tea. He looked perilously young in the early light. One day, though I knew it was bad luck, I couldn't stop myself from saying, "Do not go away again."

When he asked what had become of my mother I put down my wine and said, "She sailed for Rhodes, when you were gone, to be close to her family. She has a garden, and old friends, and says she'll die there. There are letters, now and then. I could show them to you . . ." but he shook his head and looked away.

Ice encased the city walls, and the snow filled the streets to the lintels. The fire in the hearth was all the heat in the house and it seemed that the cold had slowed time. It was like waking when I heard the first sharp crack from the ice in the harbor, its reverberation hanging in the air. I opened the front door onto a curtain of droplets cascading from the eaves, the footprints blurring in the softening snow.

The rain must have stirred him, as he started rising early and going out into the city, I knew not where. One night he told me he'd been bound by duty, in his life, but now was free, and wanted to see where all the roads led and the other side of the sea. Not yet, I said. I still need you here. You've only just come back. He nodded in agreement, or in any case he nodded, and then he embraced me, and we parted for the night, I thought, though in fact we were parting forever, and when I woke in the dark I knew he was gone.

I looked in his room, then ran into the street. The city was still deserted, and I found what I thought were his tracks in the slush and followed them to a square where all the footprints were overlaid so I guessed and ran on, knowing that if I hesitated or made a mistake he'd be gone for good, and as the sun rose the air warmed and the tracks were melting. By then there were people on the street staring at the panicked old man running through the snow in his dressing gown, and the snow was trampled into illegibility by the time I reached the harbor where green water surged in the channels through the milky, impacted ice, frozen shards and prisms flowing out to sea on the receding tide, and there was a ship, the year's first, going with them, snow tumbling from its masthead into the water. It might well have been him, up there in the rigging; I called his name, shouting to be heard over the wind, and whoever it was called back something I couldn't make out while he waved. I sat a long time on the quay watching the ship dwindling, dwindling, and then I looked away for a moment and when I looked back it was gone.

That was years ago, but even now I see him in every young man standing on a corner. Nights, I sit in my study, and when I hear footsteps on the street I run down and throw open the front door but it's always just some stranger passing by. Summers wax and wane, and in the hills the wind rattles the tall grasses around the tombs where my sons lie, and beside them are his tomb, and mine, empty, waiting.

30

THETIS

Thetis was an ocean goddess and a notorious shape-changer. She was believed to be the mother of Achilles by the Argonaut Peleus.

She lay sprawled on the cove's burning sand like a body washed up, reed-thin and frail and older than oceans. He'd seen her swim in through the high surf, unmoved by the extravagant violence of the water, and now he crept toward her over the rocks with spear and net, grateful for the waves' echoing crash and roar.

There was a seal where the girl had been, its whiskers twitching, muzzle working in its sleep. He blinked, wondering if he'd been too long in the sun, but then without transition it was a girl again. A wave broke over her; receding, it left a thin film of water on her skin, and a sand-berm by her side, embedding her, and she seemed then to be of geologic antiquity, unassailable as mountains, but her breasts, hips, sex were a woman's, so he took the last step and cast his net.

Her fingers clasped the coarse, weighted mesh. He straddled her, wrapping his hands around her thin, chill wrists. Waves washed over them as he pushed her arms over her head, his face inches from hers, breathing in the sun on her skin as he looked down into eyes like green wells.

He said, "I'm Peleus, and I want a son."

She said, "Mortal, go and find a wife."

"But I've found you, because at Delphi the Pythia said, *Take Thetis by force, and the one who springs from your coupling will exceed all in war.*"

"War," she said, stretching languidly, and her composure made him want to slap her. "I remember when the hundred-arms went to war against the gods of the mountain; the sea was cloudy for weeks and smoke blotted out the sun. It's a long time since I've seen a battle."

"When—" he started, but his hands were clutching at cold water flowing back toward the sea. From the corner of his eye he saw her crouched behind him in the breakers; as he turned he snatched up his spear and found himself facing a golden, sleekly muscled youth whose green eyes burned as he hefted a stone and said, "Was this the son you wanted?"

They stood motionless. Waves crashing, breakers' foam, water rushing over his shins, wet sand coating the lower hemisphere of the black stone in the boy's hands. When the boy moved Peleus thrust at his neck but he slipped aside so fluidly that Peleus' heart swelled even as the stone clipped his temple.

He was on his back, blood pouring down his face, a black shadow with stone lifted looming over him. "Let me go," he said. "I'm nothing to you, a man, no more. Let me live. Send me away. Forget me."

The shadow said, "I have been the vortices, the sea-foam, the breaking waves, the vast currents in the deep, the clouds in summer skies. I have been gulls riding the storm, seals swimming in the dark, sharks whose hunger draws them on like gravity. I have been everything, and lost everything, and would've gone on idling away the centuries had you not reminded me of strife's blood and joy. I'll go inland, and find armies, and the tides of war and hecatombs of soldiers will slow my long slide into nothing." A wave broke and water rushed over them. The shadow said, "What would you have named your son?"

"You will be the grief of nations,"* said Peleus, and then the stone came down.

*In Greek, "grief of nations" can be rendered as *Achilles*.

31

ACHILLES

Achilles was the mainstay of the Greek army in the Trojan War. When Agamemnon offended him, Achilles withdrew from the fight.
Achilles' best friend was Patroclus.

Achilles sits on the beach watching the waves sigh out and rumble in. Before him the sand falls away in a steep slope inscribed with the converging vees of the retreating water. He seems not to see that the tide is coming in. He has no weapon, though Troy's towers rise through the dawn mist, but they say he needs none.

Patroclus approaches diffidently, turns a weather eye on Troy, and sits down beside him, looking into his friend's face as his friend looks out to sea.

"What do you see there?" asks Patroclus. "Your mother?"

Achilles says, "I see home."

Gathering himself, Patroclus says, "The Trojans are upon us. Hector's rage is like a breaking wave scattering our men before him, and it won't be long before he and his men reach the ships with their torches and we're lost."

"There was a time, not long ago, when I would've cared. I know that, though it's hard now to believe it was ever possible."

They sit listening to the voices of the waves. Patroclus asks, "Does your mother give you counsel?"

"She wonders why I came here at all, when this war is nothing to me," Achilles says over the hiss of receding water. "And she's learned to loathe mortal men—except for one, of course, whom she loves more than all the world."

"Any mother would love such a son," says Patroclus, to which his friend says nothing.

Silence, and then Patroclus says, "Is it Briseis?* I'll give you another girl, twice as pretty, and every chief will give you another girl, for *you* are the mainstay of the army, and everyone knows it, as everyone knows Agamemnon is a fool."

Speaking slowly, Achilles says, "Men value honor, and I valued it with them, and conformed to the rules by which it's won or withheld. I went to battle joyfully and risked my life to win acclaim, and I killed many

---

*Agamemnon was forced to give up his slave-girl to placate Apollo. He claimed Achilles' slave-girl Briseis in her stead, at which Achilles withdrew from the war.

men, but then Agamemnon, in his frustration, robbed me, and I let him, because his theft revealed the whole edifice of prestige and obligation as nothing much at all, a mechanism for getting young men to shed their blood willingly on behalf of their elders who pretend to be their betters. I wish I'd never left the sea."

Patroclus asks, "Is it the helplessness?"

"Helplessness," snorts Achilles. "I could scatter Agamemnon and all his Argives like sand before a storm." Patroclus, who loves his friend, continues to look solemn. "But what would it mean? Dead men's blood soaking into sand, dead men's bodies drifting out to sea, and still the years' endless succession."

"So much for hatred, but what of love?"

"A temporary loyalty, born of shared folly," he says with a hint of a smile.

"Then lend me your armor, if you love me at all, and if you won't save us your image will."

"Why?" asks Achilles, and smiles at Patroclus with the simplicity that has always won his heart. "Come away with me. Let the war wind on as it will. All the oceans and all the world are before us. I'll show you wonders."

"I must stay," says Patroclus. "I'm not like you. I'm not remote."

Patroclus hasn't been dead an hour when a war-cry like thunder comes from the Greek camp, and Hector, whose hand is raised to finish off a Spartan, looks up;

his intended victim takes the chance to scurry away as a metallic shrieking approaches through the dunes.

Achilles surges into battle, his rage overwhelming as he bats aside nameless men and makes his way toward Hector. A path opens in the throng and Hector, who is fearless, runs to meet him, and the others will always remember that he looked like a man going not to death but to his wedding-night. On the first pass their spears pierce only air, and hope blooms in Hector's heart as a great cheer rises from the Trojans, but a moment later he lies dazed in the dust, looking up at the sun glinting on a bronze spear-point on a scoured blue sky, and then it's over.

In the hour before dawn Priam finds Achilles on the beach among the crumbling dunes. Achilles is watching the waves rumble in, sigh out; the early light is just bright enough for Priam to see the pile of blackened skulls beside him; farther down the beach are the glowing remnants of a pyre, the sprawled shadows of charred bodies. Achilles picks up a skull and uses his knife to strip off the last scraps of skin and hair as he says, "A hundred, a thousand, a million lives are not, in the balance, Patroclus. Seventy-eight. A hundred, a thousand, a million lives are not, in the balance, Patroclus. Seventy-nine." In the sand at his feet there lies a dark shape that could be a tall man's body; there's light enough to see a sandal on a splayed foot, what could be a horse-hair plume stirring in the dawn breeze, but Priam doesn't look.

"I have no weapon," he says.

"Then go and get one," says Achilles, not looking up. "Or go and get an army, but, regardless, you won't see another morning."

"I bear a ransom and hope for mercy," says Priam, kneeling in the cold sand.

"Stand, Priam," says Achilles. "You need not be humble here. In death, all are equal."

Priam says, "My son killed your friend, so you killed my son. Honor is served, and that's enough. Let it suffice. Take the gold I've brought and let me take my son away so the women can wash him for burial."

"Honor is a line in the sand, drawn by a child, blurring in the wind. I over-stepped it. So what."

"Honor is how men live. It's a road in the dark through broken country."

"Why walk a road when the dark is there, its cold fathomless and welcoming? A hundred, a thousand, a million lives are not, in the balance, Patroclus. Eighty."

"Does it ease your heart to outrage the dead? Does your lost friend feel closer?"

Silence. Then, "If honor is empty, then what? Why show restraint? Why should I let anyone live?"

"There are laws older than honor. Simple, animal things. A friend dies, and your rage burns white hot, and then it fades. You make their pyre, and send them down into the shadows to the sound of your weeping. You honor their memory, and you hope that it will fade. Sometimes you see them when you sleep." A pause. "In the end, there are other things: The first light of dawn. The rhythms of the year. A wind touching the sea. A kindness to a broken stranger."

In the dust and tumult of the battle no one saw Achilles disappear. Paris claimed to have killed him with an arrow but others said he'd simply vanished. They didn't find him when they scoured the field in the fading light, but the day had been hard on the fallen with the heat and the horses and the trampling throng. The Greeks mourned him all night, drinking strong wine by the fires that roared on the strand, and no one saw the young man who looked like Patroclus walk away on the inland road.

32

HELEN

Helen was the most beautiful woman. Her beauty sparked wars, though men meant little to her. Her husband was Menelaus, the king of Sparta. By some accounts she never really went to Troy.

It's time to be seen, someone whispers in my ear, so I walk out onto the balcony overlooking the gulf of evening as it settles over the great square where the world is waiting. It seems everyone in Sparta is crowding the courtyard before the soaring palace with the sheer white walls, and I seem so far above them as they see me and start cheering, every individual voice lost in the inchoate deep-throated roar, and that roar speaks to me, telling me they love me, that they yearn to know me and to know what it is to live in their love and my beauty, and if I could I would tell them it's like nothing in particular. And then I see not the courtyard but the volume defined by it and the palace and the encircling walls, a cube of empty air floating over the teeming masses as gulls soar through the stray light of the torches, and in that moment I'm outside myself, somewhere in the air, watching a pale woman with pale hair on the balcony lost in the white wall of the palace's immensity, her hand half-lifted in slight benediction as she looks out into space, and I want to tell the throng that loves her that I hardly know her, that when I look at her in mirrors she stares back at me with contemptuous serenity, and though I have tried to fathom the architecture of her face, the foundation of her power, her marmoreal beauty, the longer I look the less I see anything but a lightness, a blankness, as though she were insubstantial, a shadow in a bank of cloud.

They lead me to my new rooms where the maids are waiting to meet me and as I have always been happiest with other women I want them to like me but they keep their eyes on the floor as I go from each to each and praise her hair or eyes or hands though many are neither fair nor young. I say, "You are all so beautiful!" and this calms them but they're still too shy to speak to me so I ask questions about their children and about their boyfriends, and to the grandmothers I say I've heard they juggle innumerable lovers and how do they manage? They smile a little, and look up for a moment, but it isn't enough, and they're relieved when I dismiss them, and when they've gone I've already forgotten their names, and I sit silently for hours in the empty room as my mind fills with a plangent whiteness.

Then they're shaking me awake and then I'm standing on a stone floor while the maids pour steaming water over me and then someone is painting my face and when I look in the mirror I see a statue of a coldness and an antiquity that precludes contact with the women and the eunuchs who bustle around me with their eyes downcast. I'm draped in red and white and surrounded by girls in sheer dresses who look like the light of the first day of summer, and then by soldiers of whom I see nothing but their helmets' gleaming as we pass under the shadow of the gate-house and out through the iron gates and I squint in the sun at the throng in the city. The people scream at the sight of me and throw flowers and some of them try to get near to me, reaching out as though my essence were a contagion that could be spread by touch. It is, I reflect, my wedding day, and I consult myself for the appropriate emotions, whatever apprehension or giddiness or idea of success, but only find myself relieved to be engulfed in this crowd where I know just how to smile, and how, with the most fleeting eye contact, to make the people of the multitude feel seen, and I'm just present enough to manage this transaction, and while this lasts I'm happier because I know who I am and what I'm doing.

Now the crowd is so dense we're borne along down the wide streets whether we like it or not past the libraries and the shrines and the temple of Nemesis, a hateful goddess whose doors are always locked but now they hang open though no one seems to notice, for they see only me, and I peer within and over the altar there stands a statue and altar and statue are both spattered with blood as from severed arteries, and the statue has my face. I want to stop but the flow is even stronger now and impossible to resist and deep within my silences something is building that I belatedly recognize as a scream and the strangers all around are reaching for me, their hands scrabbling at my face, and I wonder what would happen if the soldiers crumpled and the crowd had its way and for a moment I would welcome this but then we reach the plaza before the temple of Hera and the mass of people opens up. Giddy in the sudden space and silence, I walk up the shallow steps to Menelaus, who is waiting at the top. He is dressed in white linen and carries a golden sword, and he flashes a wide smile with teeth which shows me how much he wants me to like him and to be impressed, and this makes me remember that I no longer know exactly why I chose him from the many essentially equivalent suitors in the first place, and as I'm thinking about this I see his smile weaken.

The echoing interior of the vaulted temple distorts the priestess's words as Hera's image glares at me with abiding ill-will and then it's over, and caparisoned horses take us back toward the palace and as we ride Menelaus won't look at me but I can see him thinking that this is it, finally, the great thing, and then I'm in my rooms lying naked on linen sheets while he kneels beside me and does what I can only describe as cataloging me, mostly with his hands but sometimes with his mouth, as though trying to confirm and comprehend my corporeal reality. I try to say something, even to touch him, but it's as though we are separated by a thick wall of glass and I'm just a shadow moving comically and erratically and perhaps not even noticeably on the other side and in any case he's still raptly taking me in and my own stillness is such that I can see what he is thinking, which is that it seems impossible that I actually exist and that he has contrived to own me. Later, when he's working away on top of me, I think of all the other suitors I might have chosen, and how they had said I was like a fire, bright as torches, my skin like sun on water, and how they'd been ready to cut each other's throats to win me, and later when my bridegroom is gone and I'm in the bath I look at the woman reflected in the still, steaming water and I ask her why she forbore to ignite the war among the suitors that was there for the kindling, for what greater tribute could be imagined to her pride or to her beauty but she only smiles slightly and stares at me in silence and even I can't look away.

My nights are an endless round of appearances in all the salons and the ballrooms and the colonnades around the gardens, and the *chef de protocol* directs my motions and even stands behind me and whispers in my ear how kind or cordial or dismissive to be to whatever dignitary or personage, and his instructions become performances, and as I'm stage-managed minutely through every dinner or ball or fête I find myself watching these affairs from a certain distance, emotion moving torpidly across my face when circumstances require a creditable show of feeling, for it isn't mine to feel but only to be seen, and to be seen to feel, and most of all to shine, and at night the great men who have sworn to ignore me struggle not to stare as I stand in the center of the ballroom while they circulate at a fixed distance, balanced precisely between desire and fear, and it seems I'm the center not just of the party but of Sparta and of all its cities whose lights are constellations revolving around me in the utterly impenetrable and soundless night.

One day I rise at dawn and go onto the balcony over the courtyard and among the receding shadows the red light reveals black writing on the courtyard wall, the letters so large that they're decipherable even at this distance and I read *Helen is a whore* and *Helen is a trap* and *Helen is a monster* and *HELEN IS THE END OF EVERYTHING* and as I read I'm laughing.

Not a month after our wedding Menelaus has ceased to call on me and I rarely see him except in court or when I pass the practice fields where he's always training with his soldiers, as relentless as a young man with no prospects but war, though he's already rich and a king and past forty. My hair-dresser tells me that they say he's no Achilles but longs to be, and by dint of long persistence sometimes comes close. I wonder if having had me his pride is sated and he's done with me for good but then one night there's a rapping at my door, and I know who it is before I open it and by the way he knocks I know he's drunk. I feel a fris-

son of revulsion when he sits on my bed so I stand
watching him with my hands folded in front of me
willing him to feel my discomfort but in fact he doesn't
notice because he's thinking.

At last he looks up with a wry face and I think he's
about to tell a joke but he says, "Do you think I'm
brave enough?" with a calf-like vulnerability that
makes me want to kick him. "Your bravery has so far
sufficed," I say. "Do you think I'm strong enough?"
he asks. "Strong enough to stay king, so far, and
strong enough to wed me," I say. "Do you think I'm as
great a man as my brother?" he says with an explosive
little laugh and I'm distressed to see tears welling in
his eyes, and I think of his brother, Agamemnon of the
thin hair and the swag belly, my sister Clytemnestra's
husband and a king in his own right, who hasn't
looked at me since my betrothal, and it occurs to me
that he's the only one who really loves my husband.
"Great enough for him to stand by you, and they say
he's a great man himself," I say, at which he sighs
deeply and topples onto his side and holds out a hand
for me so I go and lie down beside him on my own
bed and hold him though its too hot where our skin
touches and his sourness taints the air, and as his
breathing slows the silence of the room congeals into
a high shrill tone that rings in my ears as I regard
him coldly and had he opened his eyes and seen me
staring he might have taken warning but he stays
asleep and I stay there holding him, head propped on
my hand, and when the squares of sky are lightening

in the windows he rises suddenly as though rushing up out of a bad dream and though he's ragged with sleep he salutes me with glacial formality and then he's finally gone.

One night I wake freezing and the bedclothes have become sheets of ice and the walls are too close and so high that the room has become a well and the cold is unbelievable, the worst I've ever known, so bitter that I can't move and I have no choice but to accept it, to let it flow into me until I feel I've been absorbed in polar seas and the cold is almost a source of pleasure. I hug my knees to my chest and am achingly awake, my mind roaming emptily, and I know I need to leave but there's nowhere to go. In my despair I even consider calling on Menelaus, and then I think of the many men I've caught looking at me which is almost all of them and I'm aware of their proximity in the palace and in the city but to go to one and scratch on his door and watch his surprise and civil inquiry turn to need and then to slip inside and close the door would be my ruin and, worse, my degradation, and there are no options, and there never will be any options, and then I'm staring at the pale woman in the mirror by my bed as she rises and puts on a black cloak.

I follow her through the palace and out into the city where the streets read as landscape, deep canyons drowned in cold seas, and she passes by the temples and the high houses and then into the lower city where the windows are dark and the doors are gaping mouths and filth clots the gutters and then she's in the wasteland beyond the wall where outlaws and escaped slaves live in ragged huts or below tarps spread over bushes and there are eyes on her and someone whispers *You could die here* and then she's on the bank of a river-bed whose black stones glint in the moonlight and across the channel there's a bonfire and sitting before it are men's silhouettes. A trickle of dark water runs in the middle of the channel and the air smells of smoke and the sweetness of garbage as she drops her cloak and pulls off her dress and she's shivering and I can see the bumps on her skin as she splashes across the water, and her body glows in the moonlight, a white stain on a black land, and they're waiting for her by the fire, and then I lose her in the dark while I sit on the far bank watching the undulating luminous streaks on the sluggish water.

The days pass, and I lose the days, and the people love me, and I shine, and so it seems it will go forever until the moment I first see Paris. He's the most beau-tiful man I've ever seen, come to court with his brother Hector to strengthen the bonds of friendship between Sparta and Troy, he says, though I have the sense that he just likes to wander. When he's presented to me I look into his eyes and see a stillness and a distance and a contempt that mirror my own, and when I murmur the usual things what I'm really saying is, *Everything you see in me is an illusion, a brilliant surface behind which there is nothing but a slight chill*, and then later at the reception I'm standing by a fountain in a court-yard thinking of nothing much at all and then he's there beside me smiling, and though his manner is a gentleman's I think he has the soul of a thief and I can see that he is wondering if he can rob us and I take in the beauty and the grace of him and a voice whispers, *Yes. Yes, you can.*

That night I can't sleep and get out of bed when the moon goes down and sift through my possessions but find only costly baubles and make-up and all the apparatus of my endless performances and so I go empty-handed through the silent corridors to the guest wing where I find his door open and he's naked, sitting up in bed, and I can smell him, and over the next hour I wonder if how I feel now is how my old lovers felt and through it all I'm always aware that we are in Menelaus' place of strength and that fear lends a vibrancy and afterwards I want to fall asleep but he shakes me awake and asks if I will come to Troy. *Yes*, whispers a voice in my ear, and I say, "Yes," and then we are rushing through the night of the city, and I feel like a child in a story fleeing wicked step-parents, and it's a long road to the sea but already I feel we've escaped all possibility of harm and then I hear the waves breaking and see the ship's sails black on the stars. Hector is already aboard, waiting with his back to us, and then I'm watching the wake churn as my old life recedes.

The ship sings as we race over the cold sea and there's a license in our velocity and in the certainty that no one in the world knows where we are. We spend hours in the cabin, and I don't know what will become of me, and I wonder if the underlying fear is a necessary component of happiness. When we're resting I talk, as I've never really talked to anyone, and I tell him about the need of the crowd and pressure of their eyes and the men who have fallen to me, and how I wished I looked like nothing in particular, and had been no one much, and how I never wanted to be a ghost haunting my own life, and at first I think I must have misheard him when he says, "Eight times. When I've had you eight more times that will be enough, and I won't have to listen anymore." I laugh tentatively, but he says, "If you don't try my patience I might not let the sailors have you when I'm done," and I mean to say something but he smothers me with his mouth.

I have a dream that there's a woman in the room and she is very beautiful and she's saying, *I'll be the death of you and I'll have your eyes from you and I'll see your pretty face trampled in Troy's ruin.*

I wake that night with Paris sprawled beside me and slip out. On deck I find Hector standing at the prow, immovable as a figurehead, and he is the biggest man I have ever seen, and somehow the calmest. The night is silent but for the wind in the rigging and the shadow of an island looms off the bows, its breakers white on black water. I lay my hand on his wrist and stand so close that my breasts press into his arm and when he looks down at me I expect to see the changes that move through men's faces when I smile at them but he's expressionless as I whisper, "Paris has betrayed me. He is a villain, and cares for nothing, and thinks of no one, and just as he's ruined me he'll ruin you and your father and your city, if you let him. Menelaus loves his pride more than his life and he'll die before he'll let go of me. Do you want to see Troy broken for the sake of your brother's mistress?" and I feel him waver, for a moment, but he says nothing and then turns his wide back to me, and I might as well be talking to a stone, and I might as well not be there at all, and I walk away and stand by the railing, and now the island is closer on the black sea.

Though I shy away from the decisive act it comes easily to fall and the wind whips around me as I go over the side and then I pierce the sea without a sound and the salt stream is blood-warm and welcoming. I surface, kick off my dress and set out for the island, swimming underwater while my breath holds, and it's a long way but I don't seem to tire as the surging waves lift me up and lower me and the sea seems to cleanse me of everything that's passed. I look back when I hear shouting from the ship, see light flaring in the lanterns, but the ship is already relegated to the past and I swim through the surf toward the shore and my hands scrabble at the sand, and then I'm on my knees among the breakers, and then I'm walking away.

The wind blows over me and the sand warms as the sky lightens and soon it seems I've been walking here forever and there could never be another place for me. The morning light fills the gulf of sky and illuminates the white cliffs above the sand and looking back I see the ship beached a long way back and the men clambering down, but I ignore them in favor of a pale woman walking in the white foam on the narrow strand and her calm is fathomless and I wonder if she'll run or try to escape but the cliffs above the beach are sheer and crumbling and in any case the island is empty, the abode of gulls and wind, and there's nowhere for her to go. I watch her a long time and I want to ask why this is happening, and what end my fall could serve, and finally, though I haven't spoken, in a voice barely audible over the receding waves she says, *All will die, and all will die, and the pride on which they preen themselves will be their undoing, and they'll spill their hearts' blood or drink deep of black ocean or die by the hand of a woman betrayed. Paris with his girl's hands and eyes cares for nothing and will be hated by all and die shamefully, and Menelaus will be eroded by years and by pride and on the night of his triumph he'll embrace a phantom. Hector will go to fight a man he knows will beat him and before he dies he'll break before his wife and his kinsmen. Even Priam, who does a host's duty, will see his city broken and his sons burn away like grass in a fire, for Troy's towers are the kindling for their funeral pyre, and Helen is the spark.*

The beach rounds a bend and ends in black rocks, booming waves, broken surf, and there's no hope of passage. The woman eyes the cliffs but it's impossible and I say, "But I have done *nothing*, and these men are nothing to me, and their pride is nothing to me, and I have done nothing but play the roles I've been assigned," but then our conversation is cut short by the arrival of Paris and his brother and all the sailors, and though hope is gone the pale woman turns and pushes past them without the least acknowledgment and for a moment I think she'll outface them but then Paris grabs her wrists and the sailors seize her legs, and she breaks then, and tries to thrash free but they bind her hands with tarred rope and tie a halter around her neck and lead her away over the sand like a slave and she seems barely to be present though her face is as luminous as a cloud before the sun, and now they're dwindling down the beach, and Hector looks back once, and now they're indistinguishable, and now the heat haze obscures the distant sails unfurling, and now the ship is a blur on the horizon, and now it's gone, leaving me alone here, kneeling in the sand as the gulls scream and the tide comes in.

Time passes, and I sit by the shore and watch the water, and then one day at dawn I see the sea-nymphs surging through the waves and when I cry out they answer. They take me to a roofless cavern by the sea where they and their sisters lie in the sun and weave the days away. I've found my place here, and I'll never leave, but my sisters are restless and sometimes go roaming in the waters, but when the white surf brings them back with stories of a war for a woman in a city in the east I don't listen as it has nothing to do with me.

33

ELYSIUM

Menelaus was Helen's husband. After many travails, he brought her back from Troy. The gods deemed him noble so they gave him a good after-life.

I wake in the dark to the water whispering over the hull. The stars shine through the open hatch, the timbers creak, and behind everything is the sea's polyphony. The boat glides purposefully through the night, borne by the current. There's no one else aboard, and no one else for miles. I close my eyes.

When next I wake the boat has run aground and the cabin is full of light. Waves lap against the hull, and the day is passing, but I lie in my hammock watching a square of sunlight slide down the wall, over the floor and into my eyes, and I could lie here forever, savoring the slow passage of time, but instead I rise and gather my notebooks, dip nets and collecting jars.

On deck the day is blinding. The prow has incised the wet sand of one island among the innumerable islands where the tide pools punctuate the low black rock. I put on a hat made from a piece of canvas, stained with salt and tar, worn, like my ragged trousers, in grudging concession to the sun.

I shimmy up the mast but see no sails, no glittering towers, no distant mountains, just the sun's glare on wet rock and water, the glittering ripples in the channels, the incandescent white clouds like burning towers in the east, and it's just as well, I think, this loneliness, this nothing.

I pick my way barefoot over the sun-warmed rock and sit by a pool where blue crabs skulk among the translucent anemones and tiny eels flee my shadow for the safety of thick weed. With my face inches from the shining water I see the black mollusks, the branching corals, the darting fish the size of pebbles, and for a moment I seem to intuit the totality of all the lives in this pool, and their indifference to me.

I pull my net through the water and draw up a crab. It explores my hand lethargically, unalarmed by its sudden translation into air, its steps pricking my palm. I set it down on a stone where it works its palps incuriously as I draw it in the notebook dedicated to its species.

I flip through the notebook's thousands of drawings and as I go back through the months the crabs' shells become rounder, their claws longer. I have an intuition for an order in the way the animals change across the miles and the years, and one day when all my notebooks are full (there are crates of blank ones in the hold) it will be time to approach this mystery, but that day is far away, and for now I'm happy just recording life in its profusion.

In the afternoon the water's tone changes as the tide starts to rise. I move my equipment back to the boat, then stand a moment by my pool, which I'll never see again. I put my shoulder to the boat and push, my feet sinking into the sand, the boat soon bobbing in the channel, gaining way as the current takes it. For a moment I imagine letting it leave, stranding myself on these black stones among the waterways—how well I'd come to know these few pools—but then I scramble onto a low rock, leap to catch the railing, pull myself aboard. As the sun sinks the water rises and I lie sprawled on the deck with my head over the side watching the passing of the white sands, the deep urchin beds, the verdant fields of anemone.

Later I wake without knowing why. It's the last vestige of afternoon, and I'm on the verge of going back to sleep but then I see the wet footprints fading on the deck. I'm very still, listening, and there's a pressure in the air, but no sound besides the water rushing, the sails creaking in the breeze. The sun sinks, the light fades and the wind and the current carry me on my way. Lightning illuminates the cloud massifs in the east, then subsides, and I lie under the stars, waiting, listening to the sea.

That night I dream of dying—the pain, the tedium, the durationless wait. Helen sat by my bed as my delirium deepened, and at times I thought I could see through her; I asked her if she was a god, or a ghost, or something worse, but she only stroked my hair and held a cloth to my lips when I coughed up blood, which was strange, for she'd never been kind to me. "I wish I'd died as a child," I said, desperate to wound her. "I wish I'd been spared you, and Troy, and all the squandered years." Later I told her I loved her helplessly, despite everything, and always had. My breath came in a trickle and the room was getting brighter, though I think it was night, and then her face was inches from mine, the curtain of her hair secluding us. She said, "Very well. You've suffered enough," and I tried to touch her but my hand passed through her, as though she were insubstantial, no more solid than a cloud, and then she wasn't there at all. I called out for the servants but none came so I rose out of bed, which I hadn't done in weeks, and went to look for them but when I went out the door I found myself not in Sparta but in an abandoned city of white mansions and long alamedas in whose gardens I sat a long time in the sun, and then I walked down a road toward the roar of the sea.

In the morning the boat grounds on a new beach and once again I climb the mast but see no one and nothing though I look a long time. Later in the day I'm drawing a coral when a shadow falls over me and I look up to see Helen smiling down at me. I set aside my notebook and lead her into the hull's little shade and my need is such that I omit the niceties and her dress is still on as I hold her in place and my awareness narrows, then vanishes.

We doze in the shade on the sand. Eventually she touches my face and says, "You've been here a long time."

I say nothing.

"These islands aren't the end," she says. "There's an ocean, as wide as the sky, its waves like mountains, storm-wracked and fathomless, and beyond it is a new country. Even I have only had glimpses of its cities, but I can tell you the way."

"You've said as much before."

"I think I'll say as much again."

"Would you be there, in this ocean, or across it?"

"I'm not even really here."

"I'll stay."

She says nothing more but watches me as I drift off to sleep.

When I wake, I'm alone. The tide is plucking at the boat but isn't full yet so I go back to the pool, the nets, the jars, my work.

34

CLYTEMNESTRA

The wind wouldn't rise to carry the Greek armada to Troy. Agamemnon sacrificed his daughter Iphigenia to Artemis to unlock it. Clytemnestra was Agamemnon's wife and Helen's sister.

Somewhere a city is burning.

Another night on the walls of Argos, cloak clutched against the wind, staring into the dark. Across the harbor is the blackness of a mountain on whose slopes a red light sparks, flickers, flares. It's the signal-fire, cold this last decade, sending a grey thread of smoke rising into the stars' density, the radiant center of the night.

Somewhere flames surge and roil over blackening towers as the savage Greeks in the littered streets look up into raging light and screams and smoke roar upward.

The flame across the water implies a tower in remote mountains where a sentry saw a pillar of smoke and flame rise rippling over Ilium and, shaking off his torpor, put his torch to years-dry kindling. In another tower another sentry saw that blaze and so lit his own fire and so on in a succession of conflagrations surging between islands and towers over dark valleys and miles of black ocean, traveling swifter than arrows, or bad news. I imagine a shepherd drowsing with his flocks looking up in wonder at the firelight pulsing on the distant heights and not knowing, as I know, what it means, which is that Helen is in bonds again, that great Hector's bones are blackening, that Troy has gone up in flames today, that my husband is coming home.

The sliver moon's scant light reveals the white breakers on the beach where I threw his scepter into the water—it had belonged to his fathers, and was meant for his sons, too precious to risk in a war across the sea. There are the stables where I lay with three slaves in succession the night after his departure; regrettably, I didn't conceive, and so lost my chance to put a bastard on his throne. There's the white hemisphere of Agamemnon's father's tomb, where I seduced Aegisthus, the singer left behind to entertain me; I got him drunk, first—the done thing, I believe—but even drunk he said he could not possibly, that it was a matter of loyalty, of *honor*, for Agamemnon had treated him with *respect*, but I rolled my eyes and pulled up my dress and, behold, he could after all. Moonlight glows on the white columns of the temple where he slaughtered my daughter like an animal, where he cut out her bones and sent the fat of her thighs up in smoke on the altar.

The wind had been dead, the army exasperated, the becalmed armada decaying in the harbor, and the oracle had told him the gods wanted blood. He grabbed her by the hair and pulled back her head as her hands scrabbled at the knife. I was at the back of the crowd with the other wives; I would have stopped him, somehow, had I been close enough, though I'm only a woman. I thought at first it must be a mistake—had he not felt her sleeping breath on his shoulder and the softness of her hair?

Afterwards, I was going to hang myself. I had the idea she'd be lonely, down in the shadow-lands, afraid of the caverns, the dark, the other ghosts, that even then she needed me, but as I tied the rope to the rafter I remembered how he'd washed his hands in a fountain after killing her with the look of a man relieved to have put a disagreeable task behind him, and my mind ignited like dry kindling; suddenly I was empty of love, and had no purpose in life but to be his undoing. I've been waiting a long time for my husband to come home.

The wind rose on the morning after her death and they wanted to set sail while the light held so I hid a dagger in my sleeve and went to the docks. I found him shouting orders, and he didn't seem to see me as I pushed toward him through the crowd. I had a vivid presentiment of how it would feel to drive the blade into his stomach, but what if he survived the first thrust? For him, a pale scar, a new wife and an ugly story; for me, a life locked in a tiny room with my daughter's ghost whispering in the dark. Patience, I thought. Make sure of it. I caught his sleeve and said, "Come to my room a last time before you go," and made a show of carnal promise but he kissed my cheek and said there was no time. I stood on the dock, holding the knife, watching the ships dwindle.

A month after I see the signal-fire a knot of ragged ships straggles into the harbor. They look like refugees, or pirates down on their luck, but then I recognize the faded tritons on the prows. I'm already on the dock when the Argives disembark, like feral grandfathers now, and among them is a wiry grey-beard moving with the slow care of many wounds. I look away, look back, then recognize Agamemnon.

He weeps as he embraces me, the racking sobs of a man who didn't think he'd be returning. He's weak with years and battles, and his men, straggling up toward the city, are too far away to help him, and my dagger is right at hand. I couldn't have hoped for a better opportunity, but my knife-hand won't move, and then I'm wiping away his tears, telling him to come up to the castle, to come home.

I draw his bath. The steaming water glows red in the torch-light as I pour it over him into the deep marble tub. The bath slops and surges as he mumbles, hugs himself, rubs his face in his hands. He's pitiful, and it occurs to me I could care for him now, ease his way into old age and the tomb, but I think of my daughter's face as his knife touched her.

"Agamemnon," I say, my intention in my voice, and he turns sharply, glaring, and he knows, I can see that he knows, but he shakes his head and says, "Forgive me, my love. I've been too long among enemies," and I pull my lips back from my teeth as I pick up the knife.

The blade scrapes on bone and he surges out of the tub, a wave of water soaking me, the knife twisting in my hand as he tries to grab my arm but, slippery with soap, I pull free my hand and drive the knife into his flank, and then again. As in bad dreams it seems to do him no harm and when he backhands me in the face something cracks in my nose. I pick myself up as he flounders in the tub, trying to stand but falling across the rim, and then it's as though I've lived this moment a thousand times, as though I have been rehearsing it for years as I grab his hair, yank back his head and look into the pained surprise of his staring eyes as I cut his throat, and I'm shrieking obscenities, sailors' curses I didn't know I knew, and then the knife clinks on the wet tile as his life spurts away into the tub.

Something rises up in me, and it seems that this must be the end, that the world must come apart now, and I embrace this, but my heart slows and the fire that filled me fades into nothing and I'm standing here, my dress soaked, watching my husband's corpse float in the thick red water, Iphigenia these ten years dead.

PART V

DIONYSOS

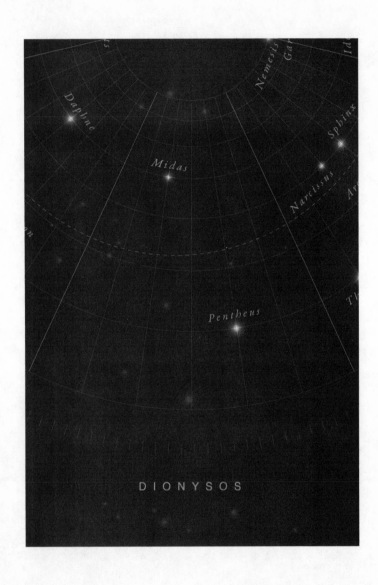

35

MIDAS

In his youth, Midas traveled with Dionysos. In his maturity, Midas invented coined money, which transformed the economy of the ancient world.

In grey hills far from home Dionysos laid his hand on my shoulder and said, "I have loved you like a brother, and I will never forget you, but here we part." A first snow was falling and my laughter plumed white but his eyes were hard and when I asked him why, he said nothing, and I was going to argue, or perhaps plead, but then I was descending through the rolling white hills, and had been for some time, though I didn't remember deciding to go.

No one and nothing but the empty air, the low clouds, the hills' swell and fall. Footprints receding behind me in the snow, and before me a white emptiness, as though I were entering a new-made country of a vast and stifling blankness. Snow swirled on cold wind as I shuffled through the thickening powder, the numb solitary hours passing. Some vapid part of me kept looking for him from the crest of each hill, behind every lonely, snow-laden oak, but he was never there, and even the memory of my time with him seemed to be slipping away, the vibrant intensity of those years reduced to a blur of wine fumes, receding laughter, firelight glimpsed in a wood. I wept without shame or restraint, and wondered if I'd already been forgotten.

Night fell and there was no moon and I'd have worried about losing the track if there had been a track but as it was I just kept walking down. The wind seemed to be saying something that I could never quite make out, and I thought of the ghosts whispering among the branches, of the maenads' songs, of the first time I saw him, shining in the firelight, with his wine-stained mouth and skewed crown of myrtle. I thought I'd walk forever but when the false dawn first lit the bowl of cloud above me I found I'd come to the end; the granite walls of Pessinus glittered on the plain below me, and past it the sun gleamed on the untranquil sea in shifting discs of gold.

I must have looked rough because the guard at the gate took one look at me and told me to get back on the road. Weary beyond anger, I said, "I am Midas, the heir. I went away, but now I'm back, so go tell my father."

"Gordius died nine months ago," said the guard wonderingly, and then he added, "Sir." I sat in the wind-lee of the wall while he hurried off to the palace. Until he got back I was uncommitted, and the momentum of events reversible, but I had nowhere else to go.

The city was smaller and shabbier than I remembered, even with the grace the new snow lent the tenements, the empty lots, the vacant husks of burned-out houses. The vizier met me in the palace's cold hall; he squinted into my face, then embraced me and asked me where I'd been. I told him the truth, though he and my father had hated Dionysos, had locked the gates against him when he came to Pessinus long ago, and I was afraid he'd speak to me as a man speaks to a boy, but he only said, "Very well—it's very well thus, and truth be told it's often thus, but that time is over now, and now your life begins." He paused, said, "The old man asked about you, at the end. I didn't think you were coming back," and I didn't have the heart to say I hadn't meant to. It was a relief to retreat to my old room, which felt like a child's but at least had a fire and a lock on the door. There had been no mirrors on the road, and as I shaved I was shocked by the gaunt stranger staring back at me and the dark pouches under his eyes, the ruined blood vessels in his cheeks, the white hairs at his temple. For a moment I was angry, as though I'd been robbed, for I hadn't expected to get older, had thought people aged because they'd made a mistake.

I woke shivering in late morning to a despair tempered only by the recollection that I was finally king and could do what I liked. I found the vizier in the treasury, the iron key to its thick door hanging on a string around his neck as he polished a golden dagger. The accumulated wealth of six generations gleamed dully in the cold light; snow drifted through the barred windows to stencil white rectangles on the floor. "I've decided I'm going back," I said, "so I'll need soldiers, and horses, and supplies for at least a year. We're leaving today, or at the latest tomorrow. I last saw him near Mount Caucasus, I think, so we have a long way to go."

"Impossible," he said. "We have few soldiers these days, barely enough for the garrisons, and in any case winter has closed the roads."

"Then I'll raise more men when the thaw comes."

"Impossible. Pessinus is poor, and the men are needed in the fields."

"I see wealth enough," I said, taking in the shining miscellany.

He regarded me flatly for a moment, and then in a measured voice meant to hide his exasperation said, "This dagger is from your grandmother's dowry; her marriage to your grandfather made Tiryns our ally, and it's for the sake of that alliance that you'll soon be marrying one of their princesses. Your great-grandfather stripped that golden cuirass from a fallen prince of Sidon—you can see the rent above the heart where he got his death-wound—and is the first root of the innumerable causes that are bringing us to war with the Phoenicians," and as his catalog went on my mind wandered until finally the force of his conviction brought me back as he concluded, "What you see here is not wealth but memory, the tangible symbols of host-right and guest-right and blood-debt left festering."

"I need soldiers more than symbols," I said, "and in any case these things have nothing to do with me."

"In fact they're you entirely," he said, slapping the iron key onto my palm and striding out the door. His certainty was such that for a moment I tried to feel some sense of coming into my birthright, but I only felt numb, and oppressed by all this cold inert mass.

That afternoon the court officials welcomed me with a succession of long speeches and the boredom was incredible as I sat there with a fixed smile and stared out the window at the drifting snow when I thought no one was looking. The iron key was cold in my hand and I thought of trying to hire men for my expedition, but the smallest bowl in the treasury was worth a village, and even if I chose to outrage the ancientry and spend my wealth I could buy nothing smaller than large estates and the friendship of kings. I wanted to walk away from the hall and go off into the hills, but I wasn't sure of the way, and winter was harsh that year, and I was afraid I'd find nothing but emptiness and snow.

That evening I visited my father's tomb, a snow-covered mound beyond the city walls. I'd hated him, but hadn't expected him to die. I tried to imagine the black cavity behind the bricked-up door, his body laid out in desiccating linen, forever staring up at a light-less stone sky.

It was still dark when they woke me for the hunt, my valet hustling me into a jerkin and pressing hot wine into my hand and then the day full of frozen sweat, horses floundering through snowbanks and far too many dogs, all culminating in the filth and misery of a dying animal. Afterwards there was a dinner where I saw men and women who'd been my friends years ago but had all somehow been transformed into stolid citizens who could talk only of their children, their horses and real property. I drank too much, but not enough to make life bearable, and that night I dreamed of Dionysos.

We were running headlong through a forest without beginning or end as the wind blew through the black branches. It seemed that our motion was tending toward some final goal that we'd always pursue but never attain, and I said, *Will it be like this forever?* and as he turned to me I noticed for the first time how young he was, how he hadn't aged at all, and the forest was silent and lightless as he said, *Everything changes, but nothing ends.* I realized I was holding the dagger from the treasury, and had been carrying it with me all along, and he looked at me with affection and real contempt as he closed my hand around the blade which then incandesced, the light so bright I saw the darkness of my finger-bones through my ember-red flesh, the after-image floating before my eyes as the dagger blurred, sagged and then melted, a viscous rain of incandescent metal dripping through my fingers, shining drops falling through the air to spatter into luminous circles on the wet black dust, and I couldn't look away as their heat and light faded, like a new constellation darkening, an image that stayed with me long after he was gone.

I woke to a glassy calm so deep I felt like I was dreaming as I walked through the silent corridors in the predawn chill. The smith answered my knock with a bleary scowl that turned to worry when he recognized me.

The bellows wheezed as he heated the furnace and filled the smithy with ruddy light. Gripping the golden dagger with blackened tongs, he looked at me again to make sure I was in earnest and then put the blade into the radiant inferno where I watched it soften and slump languidly. Among the smithy's bric-a-brac I found a mold for making bronze pommels, opened it and used a rusty nail to inscribe my name in each concavity. I couldn't keep from smiling foolishly as the smith ladeled up the molten metal, and soon I held a handful of cooling golden discs, gleaming in the firelight, unsettling in their sameness, their absence of history.

Eventually the vizier burst into the smithy, totally outraged, tears glistening in the poor man's eyes, but I couldn't seem to hear what he was saying as I watched my last golden tripod melt away.

Later my weightlessness gave way to stirrings of regret so that night I drank until my oppression lifted and then I had soldiers light bonfires and broach wine-casks in the streets. I pressed brimming cups into the hands of strangers and threw handfuls of gleaming coins high into the air. "The old world is gone forever," I shouted into the staring reddened faces, "and nothing will ever be the same!" Some didn't want to drink but I compelled them and soon, despite the cold, bare skin glowed in the firelight and cries and desperate laughter sounded in the alleys and there was a feeling that some great thing was coming. I led a procession through the streets where red wine flowed in the gutters and as we sang a paean I opened the gates. I'd thought I'd find Dionysos waiting, but in the event there was nothing there at all. The procession fell silent behind me, and as the wine wore off and the cold deepened they deserted one by one. I stayed for hours but there was only the road, the snow-bound hills, the empty night.

In spring I exhumed old maps from the palace basements and memorized the reliefs of far-away mountains and the branching lines of distant roads as though they would somehow reveal my friend's trajectory. I hired soldiers and cavalry and led them as far as the city wall but when the gates swung open I balked, appalled by the world's distances, and put it off until next year.

I'd thought the coins I spent would wind up in locked chests and buried jars but the people seemed to find money more convenient than bartering chickens for pottery and the like and soon it was the standard in the market. When I couldn't sleep I'd rise at dawn and walk through the marketplace watching my coins becoming wine, or swords, or chess, or a voyage to someplace else, and for a moment feel a stirring of the old euphoria.

I sent envoys to find news of him. The harbor was full of ships that summer, all come to trade goods for coin, and there was always one departing for the neighboring kingdoms, for the islands, for countries so distant they were little more than names.

The few envoys who returned were hollow-eyed, emaciated, deeply marked by the rigors of the world. They said he'd been seen in India, or Gaul, or Hyperborea, or that he'd died years ago and been buried long since, but none of them had set eyes on him or met anyone who had.

I decided to mount a great expedition to find him, and sent strong men to scout the wildest countries and ships to far-off seas. By then I'd learned that haste meant failure, and that action would ripen in its own good time, so I set aside years to plan and to gather money against the enormous cost. None of my forefathers could have borne the expense but my wealth had risen in a flood-tide since I'd built my mint and bought all the gold-mines in Lydia.

Years passed, and I dreamed of the day my soldiers and ships would finally venture forth but that day remained in the future. Meanwhile I found that money had made the world as mutable as water as my castles became islands, then fleets, then vineyards, then armies, and every transformation left me richer, and I came to wonder if anyone had ever had as much. I spent the days in my countinghouse, writing gains and losses in a book and managing my interests, and it seemed strange I'd once tramped across the Indus with a disreputable, hard-drinking stranger and his rabble of prostitutes.

Gold, they say, has no history, as it's endlessly reforged and melted down. This came to mind when my coins came back from distant countries, clipped and dented, my image worn past recognition. In the beginning I'd studied their erosion and scars and tried to infer their recent histories but I stopped when I realized that whatever ships, slaves, cities they had been were no more than the varied forms of a single essence, which is money.

36

PENTHEUS

Pentheus was the king of Thebes and the grandson of Cadmus. He was known for his dedication to duty. When Dionysos and his cult came to Thebes, Pentheus resisted them.

That night I see torches in the woods. I've been watching from the battlements, awaiting my moment, for Dionysos has plagued Thebes long enough. I take the ten soldiers who are at hand and lead them out the postern gate, moving carefully, listening.

The woods are eerie, like some place I've never known, though I've roamed them since I was a boy. In the distance are cries which could mean pain or pleasure or just intensity. Dionysos claims to be a god, which I don't believe, but some say he's a sorcerer, which gives me pause, and I'm ashamed to be glad my men are with me.

There's singing ahead, and pipes, and the light of a bonfire glows through gaps in the leaves. My men and I share a look, creep close, and unsheathe our swords painstakingly.

We rush in and I immediately tackle a celebrant and am about to pommel him when I see its my own castellan staring up at me, stupefied with shock and wine, and then I'm standing and sheathing my sword in disgust, for the firelight reveals nothing more sinister than a few dozen of my citizens, not young, naked but for leaves and leopard skins, stinking drunk, their fixed leers fading through puzzlement into shame. My own mother is there, the breasts that nursed me bared to the night.

One of my men drags their leader before me and throws him to the ground. He's terrified, and his cheeks have the drinker's bloom—this is no sorcerer, just an old fraud out of his depth.

"Cunt," I say, trembling—I never speak coarsely, but am outside myself with rage. "You come here? You break my laws? I'll geld and blind you. You'll *see* how we deal with charlatans in Thebes," I say, though torture is the custom of barbarians and beneath true Greeks.

He begs stutteringly for his life through tears and streaming mucus—so much for Dionysos the god. This, I think, is where right conduct has led me, to this idiot libertine mewling at my feet, to my weak-minded citizens sneaking off into the night, delightedly breaching their marriages and duty.

"Get out of here," I say, sick of him, them, all of it. "Go."

He stands, meeting my eyes for a moment—he's suddenly perfectly calm, and younger than I'd thought, and much prettier than he'd seemed, almost like a girl—and then he vanishes into the wood.

The bonfire has faded to embers, and I'm alone in the clearing—even my soldiers are gone—and the wind speaks in the branches.

There are lights among the trees. Are there lights? The wind gusts as though it will lift the forest away.

Apparently all it takes to break my men's training is the prospect of mounting a housewife in the bracken. What's surprising is that I expected better—they're just kids, and obey my law, and all laws, sluggishly. The city seems very thin tonight.

It's cold, and I can't see the lights of Thebes through the branches.

There's a leopard skin on the ground. I pick it up, wrap myself in its warmth.

Music comes from deep within the wood, high and wild.

I look back toward the dark where Thebes is. Are my people ingrates? Have I wasted my life enforcing empty forms? Leaving aside long-standing habit, do I have reason to go back?

Something is moving in the darkness, something immense, just behind the trees.

I go toward it.

PART VI

APOLLO

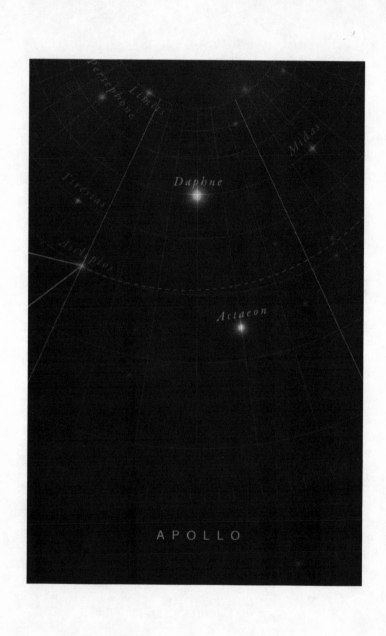

37

DAPHNE

Daphne ran laughing through the wood with Apollo on her heels. Catching her, he pressed her wrists into the trunk of a laurel but she turned her face away from his and said, "Wait." He hesitated; she was an ordinarily pretty girl, but at the peak of her bloom, and he was unwilling to violate the rules of the game.

"I'm unique," she said, looking full into his amber eyes, moved by her own daring. "There's never been anyone like me, and there never will be again, but let me live forever and I'll give you what you want."

Apollo said, "I swear by Styx* your essence will be undying."

An hour later, he vanished. She never saw him again.

As the years passed she married, bore children, grew old, buried her husband, dandled her grandchildren, and finally died.

Now other ordinarily pretty girls run laughing through the same wood with Apollo on their heels.

*Oaths made on the river Styx were unbreakable.

38

ACTAEON

Actaeon was a prince of Thebes. He befriended Artemis, goddess of the hunt and youngest of the Olympians. Apollo was her elder brother.

The sun's lassitude and salt on his lips as the white road wound on and then through the trees he heard water. He pushed into the dense pines, the darkness and the dappled light, oppressed by the noon silence and the uncanniness. He dropped his spear and bow before they could snag on the branches. There was cold water on the air and then the path opened onto sunlight on ripples and a thin girl in the green pool, white and bare, fixing him with eyes like pale moons.

She swept a handful of water at his face, and he watched stupefied as the sun caught the droplets in the air; the cold was shocking, and welcome, and when he'd wiped his eyes he saw she was smiling at him, and then she ran out of the water and into the trees that shivered in her wake. He plunged after her, floundering across the pool and then running through a winding tunnel of heat and shadows, ignoring the boughs that lashed his face, but she stayed ahead, a flash of white among the branches.

He found her sitting in a clearing, wearing a ragged tunic, rocking back and forth in the sun. A bow and quiver lay by her hand. *I'm going hunting*, she said. *You come hunt too.* He stood in the sun thinking, then said he couldn't, he was due home soon, but his words lacked conviction, and then the clearing was empty.

They became good friends. It was summer and they swam in the streams and coursed over the bare hills and through the haunted woods and saw sunlight even in their dreams. In the deep places in the mountains they sometimes heard his brothers calling and the belling of their dogs but never saw them.

They drifted away from Thebes and into the wild. She showed him a desert where the wind had scoured the stones into the shapes of clouds and they scrambled up the rock-faces of rough granite to perch high on the boulder-piles and listen to the wind and the ravens. She showed him her cache of ancient arrowheads, some crumbling and verdigrised, others razor-sharp and new; she said she'd been collecting them from battlefields since the first wars among men.

They stalked animals through a deep forest whose name he never knew. She'd stop him and they'd listen to the sighing branches and then to barely audible motion in the distant brush. They inched toward their unsuspecting prey over the course of hours and the boar or hind had to be close enough to touch before she finally said, *Run*, her low voice filling the hush, and the animal would startle and crash away into the trees as they pursued with drawn bows and killed it with their arrows.

One day they crested a hill at dusk and below them was a city in a valley of light. It was the biggest city he'd seen, though it was in the middle of the desert and the heat was only bearable at night. He worried they'd stand out with their torn clothes, tangled hair and sunburned faces, but she told him not to mind it, and the adults moving among the palaces and the casinos hardly seemed to see the ragged pair of children watching the flute girls and the drunks and the fireworks over the theaters. It was as though the true life of the city were hidden behind a veil through which they peered with detached interest, much as they observed the lives of animals, and when they were done they lay in a culvert at the city's edge and watched the stars.

In the silence of desert places there was nothing to do but tell stories. She told him about the dawn of time, the old things lingering in the shadows of the world, and how her brother knew the future, while he, having nothing else to offer, invented stories about himself and what he'd do.

One day he said he had to go back. Why, she'd said, for there's time enough, but he said he had to, that he'd been gone too long and they'd be missing him, and then he walked away. She didn't think he meant it and waited for him in the desert and then in the forest and finally she looked for him in the hills around Thebes, but he was gone, and the woods were a waste without meaning, the site of the reckless pursuit of things she didn't need, but it was summer, and she'd lost friends before, and she forgot him.

Years moved like waves over the world and when next she saw him she was swimming in the green pool in the forest outside Thebes. There was a crashing in the undergrowth and when he emerged from the trees she saw that he was taller and wider and had muscles like a wrestler's, the kind to slow him down. Waist-deep in the freezing water she smiled up at him and for the first time felt his eyes' pressure.

They sat on the bank and spoke of their old hunts and the places they'd been. He told her about his importance in the city and the women who admired him, and then the conversation flagged, and they sat there in a silence she tried to interpret as companionable. She saw a strange dullness in his eyes and then he was on top of her, pushing her into the moss, his mouth at her breast.

She writhed like a fish and slipped away, leaving him on hands and knees trying to apologize but she'd already disappeared. He was looking for motion in the gaps in the foliage and calling her name when he heard a bowstring creak behind his ear. *Run*, she said.

PART VII

DEATH

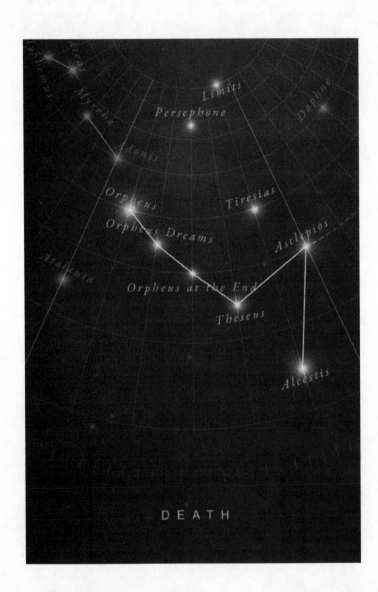

LIMITS

Zeus, Poseidon and Death were brothers. After de-feating the giants they had the disposal of the world.

Zeus, Poseidon and Death met to settle the limits of their kingdoms.

Zeus said, "I claim the islands in the seas."

Poseidon said, "Take the islands. I claim the seas around them."

Death said, "Take the islands and the seas. I claim the emptiness within them."

40

PERSEPHONE

Persephone, a cyclical goddess, was sometimes queen of Hell.

It's night now and raining harder, the rain drumming on the roof and water streaking the windows that reflect the firelight and the blurred crowd of celebrants through which I see Death passing through the garden. I know him at once, though he can't have been invited, and the young bloods pressed around me sense my abstraction and talk the louder, but Death, pale and distant, holds my eyes, and I feel my old life start to recede.

I scan the crowd for my mother but can't find her and then I hear her laughter rising high and sharp over the crowd's babble and in that moment I push past the startled beaux and staring ladies and out into the garden where the hard rain stings my face and the wind tears the white trees but there's no one there, and then I glimpse him through the thrashing branches. As I

pursue him the garden gives way to stone cliffs and
fields of talus falling steeply toward the churning
clouds that ring the mountain, and for a moment I feel
the isolation of my mother's high house on this peak
like an island in an ocean of storms. I plunge down the
path, finding my footing through luck and intuition,
but he's a black shadow on the wet rock below me and
then disappears into the clouds.

My legs are trembling as I descend into the white
blankness. A nocturnal hunter howls high above me
and for some reason the despair and fury in its cry
make me think of my mother saying Death was of an
ancient family, his lineage as great as ours, but that
he'd broken with them long ago and now was never
received, and the hatred in her voice had overwhelmed
her carefully mannered gentility.

The rain picks up as I come down out of the cloud
and the sun is rising when I reach the hills and I think
of my mother's house and the maids singing as they
light the fire for my morning bath but then I see him
in the distance and forget about home.

It's the first time I've left the mountain. I'll be all
right, I tell myself, repeating the words as I walk down
the road through a world that's emptier than I'd expected, seemingly full of nothing but the silence of
the woods and in the evenings the lights of homesteads
in the valleys. I lose him for days at a time but whenever I'm on the verge of giving up I see him watching
me from a hilltop.

The days get colder and at night I take shelter in

haystacks and ramshackle barns and as I shiver I remind myself I'm having an adventure. I think of Death often but more often I think of nothing as winter settles in and snow subsumes the fields and the orchards bear nothing but ice, and at some point in the hazy insupportable days I stop noticing the cold. My pride won't let me go knocking at farm-house doors, and when I'm exhausted I remind myself of the hardness behind my mother's elegant airs, of her unending critique of my manners and mores, of her inflexible ambition to wed me to "some plausible boy from a reasonable family, and if they aren't quite us, my dear, well, who is?" Sometimes at night I think I hear her calling me and abandon whatever nest I've made to hurry on for she's relentless and has no interest but me in the world.

Winter deepens and it seems a long time since I've seen the sun or even firelight and the snow on the road is as high as my waist when a witch finds me weeping at a crossroads. She lifts my chin with a gnarled finger and asks, "For whom do you weep?" to which I say nothing.

She says, "All women are my sisters, and through the grace of Hell's queen I have power over men, so tell me his name and he'll open his arms for you."

"Swear it," I say, and she does, on the Styx and on her mistress, but when I do tell her she falls silent and I have to press her on her oath before she finally leads me into the wood where she roots in the snow for a waxy green plant with red berries.

"Eat six," she says, "then walk toward the sound of the river, and you'll find the way to him." My stomach clenches but I keep the berries down as I wallow through the snow toward a roaring that grows louder as the light fades and my eyes are drawn to the shifting boughs, the insubstantiality of the snowy verdure, and I come out of the woods by a cave-mouth and a black river.

The sound of water follows me down into the cave as I leave the light behind and then I'm groping my way. I'm in a tunnel that goes on for miles and when the walls finally recede I put my hands out before me like a somnambulist. No sound but the rasp of my footsteps on sand, and no light at all, but somehow I sense vastness. I could be going in circles—in any case, I walk a long time, and then my outstretched hands find his face.

I say something but my words disappear like coins dropped in a well, and he never speaks at all. I know him by his hands on me, his cold breath, the contours of his face. He holds my hand as we ford freezing rivers in the dark. We lie together on the coarse, dry sand and I trace his body with my fingertips and try to remember that somewhere the sun is in the sky.

Sometimes his affairs call him away and I'm left to wander listlessly through his kingdom of absences. I clutch my arms to my chest, and tell myself it was worth the sacrifice as I aimlessly push on. Sometimes there are ghosts but they're often confused, some-times mistaking me for their queen, and it's a black hour like every other when I hear someone calling my name and then I say, "Mother?"

Then she's clutching me, enveloping me in her heat and strength. "You're leaving, right now," she says in a voice of iron, and I weep helplessly into her shoul-der, for my lover is a stranger to me, and I want to go home.

"We can't," I sniffle. "The surface is miles away, and the passage is dark."

"You're going."

There's a presence in the darkness and Death says, "*She stays*," in a voice like the rattling of dry stones. "*She came willingly to my kingdom, and the number of my subjects will never decrease.*"

"I will stay. I will stay in her place," my mother says. I mean to tell her not to, that I won't let her, but she gives me a last kiss and pulls her hand out of mine.

"Are you there?" I cry, and listen, but there's no sound, no sense of motion, and then in the distance I see a faint grey light and feel the faintest breath of wind. If I were brave I'd stay but my courage fails and I take the chance she's giving me.

I go up through miles of tunnels and then see a loz-enge of pale blue sky. Walking into daylight is like ris-ing out of water; winter is gone, and I lie gratefully in rank grass and flowers, the sun hot on my skin. It's quiet, but the quiet isn't absolute—birds chatter, wind whistles through the branches, the river burbles. A plume of smoke rises from the cave-mouth, furls in the wind, dissipates.

Having nowhere to go, I go home. I'm sick in the mornings, and tell myself it's nothing, but by the time I see the mountain I'm starting to show.

I can see from a mile away that the house is abandoned. I kick down the front door and within find decay—the filthy solaria are full of glaucous light, the garden choked with crow's nests and weeds. The ballroom is a wreck, the pillars cracked, shards of glass ankle-deep on the floor. There are the basements and galleries deep in the mountain but I leave these locked and keep to the rooftop arcades where I watch the sun and moon rise and the clouds coming in over the sea.

I clean a few rooms and cede the rest to dust and spiders. As my term approaches even this tiny domain is too much to manage until the day one of my mother's maids shows up on my doorstep. I open the door a crack and peer out cautiously but she curtseys and bustles in, taking up her work without a fuss or, thankfully, any questions, and a week later the next maid arrives, and it isn't long before the house is full of life again. I doubt my right to be there, but they treat me as mistress as a matter of course.

I give birth in the bed where my mother bore me. The maids take my daughter and wash her and then put her in my hands; I kiss her, hush her, give her my breast and swear that what happened to me will never happen to her, that she'll have the life I threw away and never be lost in the dark.

I raise her in my mother's house, which I have to learn to think of as my own, and it's not long before she's chasing butterflies among the rooftop colonnades, planting delphinium in the garden, lying in the sun and watching the waves roll in on the sea. She grows up tall and strong, and though I'd expected my vitality to flag as hers waxed I find I'm only growing stronger, my muscles hard as iron, my will absolute.

I never let her leave the mountain. We receive only the best people, the scions of ancient families full of grace and light; we are never at home to bounders, social climbers or mortal kings.

One day when she's still a child but only just, she solemnly informs me of her intention to marry her nurse's son. I say, "My dear, I'm very sorry, but that's not possible. I don't mean to be a snob but we really must find you some suitable boy of plausible family, and if they aren't quite us, my dear, well, who is?"

As her beauty grows so does my strictness for I'm determined to see her into a good marriage and the happiness I discarded whether she likes it or not, but as though intoxicated by her own bloom she fights me at every step—she won't be polite to guests, won't come down to dinner, won't anything. She says she wants to see the world. "And what will you find there?" I ask her. "I'll know when I get there," she says. "You'll only know when it catches you," I say. I have to compel the ingrate child to attend the balls that are her best opportunity to meet our sort of people, and am cursed for my pains.

One night there's a party in the ballroom by the garden to which I had to threaten to drag her. The ballroom is full of candle-light and dancers and it seems even her sullenness must be overcome. The heirs of great houses flock around her, but even from across the room I can see she can't be bothered to be civil. A grizzled Sea-lord accosts me with an anecdote and I look away from her for a moment, and when I look back she's gone, the pouring rain framed by the open garden door.

My cry snuffs candles, shatters windows, cracks stone. The Sea-lord asks something and puts his massive paw on my shoulder but I send him sprawling and then I'm in the garden but she's already gone and then I'm running down the path through the clouds into the hills but I can't find her anywhere though I look for her all that night and the next day and the next. The world is wide, and there's no sign of her, but my one certainty is I'll never let her go.

One night I'm in the mountains of Thessaly and see a fire down in a valley and hear someone calling my name. I find a granite altar before a bonfire, still wet with the blood of a black heifer, and once again the witch lifts her voice to call to me.

"I hear you, little sister," I say, still beyond the fire-light, and she starts violently and looks for me in the dark.

"I'm looking for my daughter," I say. "Have you seen her?"

"How would I know her?" she asks, her voice shaking, and the way she speaks is strange, almost incantatory, like she's performing a ritual.

"She looks much like me," I say, stepping into the firelight.

"I know her. I've seen her. She sought her lover."

"His name," I say, and on the slope above us talus clatters down the mountain.

The wind whistles in the rocks and whips the fire and finally the witch says, "Death is her lover," as I knew she must, and I cover my face with my hands.

I find the cave by its plume of sulfur and walk down into the dark. The way seems shorter this time, and soon I'm wandering in the endless night of his kingdom, calling for her, and at last I hear a small voice say, "Mother?"

I rush toward her, my hands finding her face and thin shoulders. "You're leaving, right now," I say as she collapses into me, weeping, my foolish, lovely girl, whom I would have spared this.

"We can't," she says. "The surface is miles away, and the passage is dark."

"You're going."

Then there's a pressure in the air and Death is with us. "*She stays*," he says in his raspy little voice. "*She came willingly to my kingdom, and the number of my subjects will never decrease.*"

I lunge for him and catch his wrists and he's as strong as night but I won't let him go no matter how the struggle hurts me, and in his ear I whisper, "Let her go, or I will make you let her go," and he says,

"*None leave, and none compel me*," and then I bend the fullness of my strength against him, and he gives perhaps an inch, which is little enough but I'm happy to think how even this must hurt his vanity, and then I can move him no more. My daughter is crying hopelessly. I say, "I will stay. I will stay in her place," and he softens, and our melee becomes an embrace, and he says, "*I've missed you*," but I'm watching her shadow move toward the grey light where the way lies open.

41

ORPHEUS

Orpheus was the best singer. Even the gods admired him. Eurydice was his lover.

We rarely spoke, but we were always together. We were young then, Eurydice and I, and had no care, and slept where the night overtook us. Every day I woke at dawn, for I loved her best asleep, with the light making geology of her hips' and thighs' curvature. When I was with her my voice was a bird startled into flight. I gave concerts, and they flocked to hear me, immortal faces sometimes shining in the crowd, but I sang only for her.

One night I dreamed of a cave-mouth where we stood eye to eye as she pulled her hand from mine; the sun lit her eyes for what I knew was the last time and then she turned and walked down into the dark. I woke beside her on the grass, found the pulse in her neck and watched her as the night passed, but was uncomforted, for the dream had the feeling of prophecy, and I could only think of the first day of all the days I'd wake alone.

In the morning I told her I'd be away for a while but wouldn't tell her where I was going. It was a long road to Thrace and the wild country where Death had his temple. Rain sluiced through the rotting roof and there was no one to mend it for Death disdains sacrifice and is deaf to pleading.

I tuned my lyre in the lee of shattered pillars and sang of finding her with every morning and losing her with every night, how this would go on till I lost her for good. I'd never sung better, and when the light had faded I felt someone standing behind me in the dark. Death said, "*Leave off. Enough.*" I let a last note dissolve in the air and then said, "O king of a bleak country, you rule ghosts enough. They say you grant no favors, but don't take Eurydice away."

"*Why should I spare her, her among all of you?*"

I said, "Without her, the world is empty, and my mouth is shut."

Death looked like he was going to argue but then said, "*I will never take anything you love.*"

She might have been asleep. Her skin was unblemished, soft, cooling. I held her head on my lap, stroked her forehead, sang to her as the minutes passed. The wedding guests circled us, speaking in low voices, but I ignored them until the sun was setting and I took her hand, which had clutched the grass, and saw the blood pooled under the skin of her palm like a wet vermilion stain. Some cousin said, "She's gone," and laid a hand gently on my shoulder but I threw him off and said, "Death has robbed me, and he will pay."

The wedding guests stood over her body, watching me walk away.

I went back to Death's temple but he wasn't there. I found oracles and asked the way to his kingdom, but they only spoke in tongues, or sent me off to explore shallow caves that held nothing worse than bats and cold water, or said I'd find him soon enough.

I wound up in a city, a great metropolis where it was easy to disappear. I was out of money and felt empty and when I made myself pick up my lyre my fingers were numb. I didn't want to see old friends, or anyone at all, so I slept in forgotten basements, in the warrens of rotting factories, in the alleys behind stately houses where I'd once been a guest, and sometimes in those abandoned, in-between places a chill lingered in the air where Death had passed by.

Crowds grated on me and I was only calm in the dark places beneath the city, the cellars and underground stairways with their quiet, graffiti and dust, and the corridors there went on forever, branching and re-branching endlessly, drawing me ever downward, until I forgot the blinding glare of the sun. Now and then I stumbled on other outcasts sitting in silent congeries, staring into scrap fires in deeply buried smoke-filled rooms. Sometimes I sang for them—not the classics, but new songs of loss and rage and distance, and some of the songs had no words. Though they were outcasts and pariahs they attended raptly, and sometimes there was a tall figure standing in the deep shadow, listening, but he never spoke and I never saw his face.

I drifted deeper into the service tunnels, the ventilation shafts, the forgotten sub-basements, and I was alone absolutely, weeks slipping silently by. I'd forgotten Eurydice's voice, though I still remembered her face, and she seemed like someone I'd known in a dream. Sometimes I heard a faint singing, filtering up through a grating or rising tinnily from a pipe, and it could almost have been one of my songs, blurred and echoing, but it always faded quickly and I could never be sure.

I found a store-room carpeted in broken glass and in one wall my scrap of candle illuminated the mouth of a narrow chute with TO THE UNDERWORLD scrawled over it in red paint beside a crudely drawn arrow pointing down. From the chute came a faint clattering as of distant machinery. Resigned, I felt my way in.

The shaft was furred with dust, and very steep, and when I slipped I slid headlong, and wondered if I'd find her waiting at the end. My velocity would have been alarming if I'd been able to see, but presently the chute leveled out and dumped me onto a stone floor. It was pitch black—I listened, hands extended, palpating the dark. I stood there a long time, everything perfectly still, and then said, "Is anyone there?"

Death said, "*I'm here.*"

"I've been looking for you a long time."

"*I heard you singing in my kingdom's upper reaches. This isn't a place for living men, but for your music's sake I've blessed and kept you.*"

"You broke your promise. You swore you wouldn't take her."

"*I broke no promise, but I'll break my own law to give you what you want,*" and beside me someone choked and inhaled raggedly. "*Take her, if you want her,*" said Death, "*and lead her into the sun.*"

I lit my candle and saw the mouth of a passage going up and Eurydice standing beside me. I was afraid she'd turn to ash and shadow when I touched her but her hand was warm and solid.

As we climbed she started talking. She'd never spoken much before, a reserve I'd attributed to serenity, or perhaps to wisdom, but now it seemed she couldn't stop, as though she were defying death's silence, and soon I knew her better. She was simpler than I'd thought, simpler than I'd have thought possible; she was kind enough, but understood nothing; she liked that I was famous, and was happy to be with me again, but only mildly, in the accepting way of animals. She'd been less a lover than a trope of literature.

The tunnel emerged into a shallow cave. The fields beyond the cave-mouth shone in the sun.

"Wait," I said.

We spoke quietly in the shadows.

We clasped hands, and then she pulled away. I tried to read sadness in her empty eyes but found nothing. I watched her back recede into the dark.

Here, I thought, is matter for a song.

42

ORPHEUS DREAMS

Orpheus dreams he's drifting down a river. With him in the water is everyone he's ever known—his parents, his brother, the old man who taught him the lyre, the boy whose name he's forgotten who lived down the road from the house he now sees on the low bank passing by. The river rings with their cries, splashing, laughter, and the water is warm, and a torpor settles over them as the hours pass, and finally they float on in silence. He floats on his back, the sun hot on his face, and closes his eyes.

When he opens them again he's left everyone behind. There are voices upstream but no one close by now, and he wonders how he could have lost them so quickly, but then he sees Eurydice and forgets them. She hasn't seen him yet, and she's younger than he remembers, floating along like someone drowned. For a moment he can't bring himself to make a sound and risk shattering her repose, but then he swims toward her, and when he takes her hand she returns the pressure, turns her face to his, opens her eyes.

They drift together, their clasped hands his sole point of reference. They pass through dappled light filtering through overhanging branches, the stillness of silent pools. There are others somewhere, splashing and calling, but their voices are faint and getting fainter. He maneuvers through the water to embrace her, and they hold each other as the current carries them along.

The afternoon winds on, and he wants nothing to change, but then the river's voice rises. He hears white water, and the current strengthens, and then he's pulled under for a moment and loses her. He fights back to the surface, gasps, sees her just out of reach, but the water is swift now and the gap widens. She watches impassively as he struggles against the flow. He's determined not to give up, but his shoulders burn and he's soon exhausted. The river pulls him ahead, and as he rounds a bend he calls out to her, but the rapids submerge his voice. It doesn't seem possible that this parting could be forever, and he tries to swim back to her, fails, rests, tries again, but he makes no progress, and she doesn't appear, and finally he gives up and drifts.

The river is lonely now, no noise but swift water and strangers shouting far away. He lets the flow carry him along, not caring where he goes. He sees his parents then, far ahead; he calls out, but they don't seem to hear him; he calls again, louder this time, and at last they look up, wave, shout something he can't hear, and then they vanish behind a bend, lost for good in the river's wending.

Floating on his back, he watches the branches pass overhead, the leaves shadows on the greying sky as the rain sifts down, and he tries to discipline his mind, to think only of the water, of the image of blown leaves and rain falling toward him, for this is the present, and he has nothing else, and time seems suspended, but then in the distance he hears a roaring. He turns in the water and raises his head as he rounds the last bend; the trees are thinning on the banks, and there's the ocean, and before him the river disappears under a white line of breakers. He thinks yes, of course, it couldn't end any other way, every river must come to the sea.

There's someone on the shore, a woman, watching him, and he can't see her face, but she waves to him, is waving still—goodbye, goodbye!—as the low ragged waves engulf the river's smooth flow, and at the point of transition he feels the rip take him, sees the tall waves rising, starting to fall.

43

ORPHEUS AT
THE END

After Eurydice, Orpheus became a recluse. He re-
jected the maenads of Dionysos, who killed him.

The dark wood gave way to a river pouring into the
sea, and there was no farther to go. He built a shelter
out of fallen branches; it let in the rain, but poverty
was an old friend, and the cold cleared his mind as his
voice twined around the rain drumming on the leaves,
the gusting wind, the blurred roar of the water.

He'd thought he'd escaped Hell unscathed when he
left the cave-mouth for the sun. He'd gone to Athens
and practiced his art and been much caressed, but it
wasn't long before he learned to despise his audience
for applauding music whose tiny flaws and underlying
monotony were readily apparent and agonizing to his
ear, and he'd despaired, knowing he was still lifetimes
from real mastery. He'd sought out old friends but they
seemed to be speaking across a gulf, and he'd been unmoved as he watched the city's life go by, and finally
he'd left.

In the mornings he woke on the cold ground, grateful to escape the dreams of Eurydice, how he'd wasted
her life, how he'd never loved her at all, of her face as
she turned away. Sometimes he thought he should seek
her out again, beg her pardon and stay with her in the
dark.

At night he heard the ghosts whispering, saw the
shadows of the predators creeping through the trees
and sometimes torchlight flickering through the
branches, but still he went walking in the wood. He
swam in the black water of the frigid river and sat with
his eyes closed in a lightless meadow, listening to the
sigh and blowing of the wind, to the world's subtle
music, to the rush of his blood.

One night by the riverbank he heard someone coming through the wood. He knew it wasn't a safe place,
and he could have run, but he was certain the women
rushing out of the trees had nothing to do with him.
When he started to sing again their heads snapped up.
They gathered around him, staring, clad in thorns and
mud and crowns of vines. When he turned his back on
them one of them screamed, her voice as raw and
ragged as a child's, and threw a stone that hit his head.

There was a moment of pain and then he didn't
want to move. The grey sky through the black branches
seemed unreal and remote—then they jostled him and
he saw the wet sand inches from his eyes. He felt what
might have been teeth, and then he felt what might
have been a knife, and then he was just cold. Someone
put a hand over his face, to protect his mouth and eyes,
he thought, and he focused on that as the women

worked, and was grateful, for with that hand there it seemed that nothing very bad could happen, and in any case his body had become nothing but a formless chill. Then the women were gone, their cries receding into the wood, and as the hand came away he looked up into Death's face.

He smiled, or tried to, and said, "So this is the end. I wonder if Eurydice will forgive me," but Death gravely shook his head. The sky was lightening then, enough for him to see the rags and tatters of flesh that were all that was left of some dismembered animal. Death said, "*No. This is not the end,*" and caressed his hair, and for a moment Death couldn't meet his eyes.

Orpheus laughed and said, "I've seen enough now, and am due in your kingdom."

"*You have seen next to nothing,*" said Death. "*There are billions of years yet to come.*"

"It's time for me to die."

"*I promised never to take anything you love.*"

"But nothing is left."

"*You can still sing,*" said Death. "*And now there are no distractions. Now there will never be any distractions.*"

"For whom would I sing?"

"*I'll always be listening,*" said Death, and picked him up and put him in the river.

The water closed over his eyes and filled his mouth and he tried to say forget the promise, forget everything I've ever said or sung, don't bar this last door against me, this is more than I can bear, and then he thought he heard Death say, "*But you will bear it.*" He panicked, screamed, sobbed, but it made no difference, and he drifted along. He implored Death to take him, prayed to all the gods who'd ever loved him, called upon his mother, his father, the god of the river, but no one answered, the river quickened and he tumbled on.

Apathy then, and time passing. The worst having happened, there was nothing left to fear, and he closed his eyes. Dawn came, the sand grains shining as they drifted through the bars of light in the water, the riverbed slipping by, but Orpheus slept and dreamed of nothing.

On waking he panicked because his nose and mouth were full of water, then panicked again because it didn't matter. The current was stronger then, and the taste of the water changed as he floated out into the sea.

He drifted for days, praying incessantly for release, reciting his prayer over and over, the words fading until it was little more than music, a sound stripped of meaning reflected in his mind, and he kept changing it until the music was right, which pleased him, and perhaps pleased the gods, but they, having ignored him, were of less concern.

Days, he watched the sky—the gulls flying by, the mutable clouds, the sunlight distorted in a few feet of water, and felt like he was learning to see. Nights, he listened to the ocean.

Finally he let go of everything—his grief, his prayer, even Eurydice. Drifting, knowing he'll always drift, he starts to sing.

44

THESEUS

In his youth, Theseus killed the Minotaur. Later he was king of Athens. He feared no one, not even the gods, and thought there was nothing he couldn't do. His best friend was Pirithous.

White stars burn in empty immensity over the sparse snow on the frozen earth. As my shivering subsides I want to lie down and turn my face to the sky but instead I clutch my spear in my hands, force my eyes open and take a step forward, and then another, though my mind feels vacant and the only certainty is I've been lost a long time.

Fire-light blooms before me and in front of the flames is the shadow of a man who is calling my name and I realize I know him. Slurring despite myself, I say, "Pirithous?"

He sits me so close to the fire that the heat and light are almost unbearable. Snow-flakes disintegrate in the glowing air over the rippling flames and somewhere in the distance I hear a river rushing. Still freezing despite the fire's heat I say, "I hadn't thought it could be so cold."

"It will be warm when the sun rises," he says, smiling across the flames.

Silence then, as I hold my hands to the fire, calmed by his presence, and as the chill finally subsides a shard of memory rises and I say, "I was hunting."

"It will keep," says Pirithous. "Hunt tomorrow. For now, stay here with me."

He hands me a wine-skin from which I drink greedily, the wine like hot blood as it pours down my throat and as I drink I remember more and I look up and say, "I know who I'm hunting. It's Death who I'm hunting."

His face hardens and he says, "These words are luckless. Drink and hold your tongue."

Bitterness wells up and my words come in a flood as I say, "What good this fire, this river, this bitter night, when we're caught in another river bearing us to a black sea from which there's no returning?"

"There's good in friendship," Pirithous says quietly, "and in women, and in wine, and in war's intensity. There's good in a respite from a long road."

"Friends perish, and women and wine are used and soon forgotten," I say. "To make war on men is to fight shadows to no purpose, for Death is the only real enemy."

"Enough. My friend, no more," says Pirithous, almost begging me. "Leave it for morning. For now, we're here together; let that suffice."

"Do you think I can't do it?" I ask, voice shaking. "Do you think I'm not equal to the task? I was just a boy when I came back to Athens with the Minotaur's blood on my hands, when no one expected me to come back at all, and I have yet to meet the man who is my equal. I scorn the powers of the night, and my will has no limit, and I see nothing worth having but life without end."

He suddenly seems weary, the fire-light seething redly on his face as the wine-skin falls from his hand into the ash and something has gone out of him as he says, "You always tried to do too much. But who could blame you? From your first youth you were a conqueror and you learned early on that defeat is the province of others. You shone in those days, but were too much alone, for you could only ever speak of your ambition and of your victories, and the boys who would have been your friends shied away from you, and for all your excellence you had no one but me.

"We were always together, so much so they said we were one person, and we seemed to be untouchable. We defeated famous men and hunted in the back-country and razed the walls of proud cities, and in the end we always came back to Athens unscathed. We went on like that for years, and it seemed we'd go on like that forever, and even when the grey was spreading through our beards you swore it meant nothing, that age couldn't touch us, that our true selves would never change.

"And then there was your third wife, that little Cretan girl, and what happened with your son . . ."

"Hippolytus," I say, choking back a sudden spasm of grief.

"We left Athens then, at your insistence; you needed an adventure to put bad luck definitively in the past. Do you remember the hunt for the black bull of the mountain?"

"Yes," I say, though in fact I remember only a long sweep of white horn and black mass gliding through the shadows of the wood.

"We went to Delphi, before we set out, and the oracle told you to go home—a happy old age was waiting, she said, but only if you went back to Athens and stayed. You laughed, calling her a timid old woman, and we rode away.

"We climbed the mountain and on the heights there were rows of scars on the tree-trunks higher than a man could reach. We found the black bull in a clearing; he was big as a hill and had a man's face, and he was terrified, when he saw us, and ran in a panic as we pursued him through the broken light. He wept when we brought him to bay, and then he charged us. It was like facing an avalanche and as he bore down on us I went numb and seemed to be watching myself from someplace far away but you went straight for him so I could only do the same. We had one chance, and cast our spears at the same moment; mine struck his thigh but yours pierced his heart and we leapt aside as he blundered past a few paces, then looked at us over his shoulder reproachfully and collapsed. You were shaking and your war-cry tore the air but ceased abruptly when you saw that I'd been cut."

"Be silent," I say, but my voice is weak and he doesn't listen.

"The wound was a shallow seam of blood beading, but by evening my shoulder was red and swollen, and when you carried me through the gates of Athens my arm was inflamed to the wrist and I was delirious with fever and even when I was awake I thought I was dreaming. You held my hand for hours and put a wet cloth to my brow and swore I'd be fine, that you'd see to it. You promised the doctors gold if I recovered and exile if I died, and the black smoke of burnt offerings darkened the skies above the temples. You were with me through the night as I thrashed and mumbled, and around midnight I was finally still, at which your heart rose for you thought the tide had turned, and for the rest of the night you ignored the doctors when they asked you for a very quiet word. Only at dawn did you finally admit that you were alone, and had been for some time, that the hand you held was cooling."

I rise in disgust and I'd hear no more but I have nowhere else to go in this sea of dark. He says, "My funeral pyre was by the sea. You built an altar to my ghost and slaughtered hecatombs until the sand was sodden with blood and the people said you'd squander your wealth on my memory but then on the third day when black flies were thick on the pools of gore and even the poorest citizens had more meat than they could carry you walked away.

"You wanted nothing more to do with Delphi but had heard of another oracle, one hidden among the unnavigable deltas of Lernea and said to be more sympathetic to men. For days you picked your way over the ephemeral sand-banks among the tide-channels where flies swarmed and gulls clamored until one night you heard singing. You followed it to a low cave of wet sand, and in it, half-buried, found a man's head, eyes closed, voice lifted, his neck ending in a ragged, bloodless wound. When he finished you blinked back tears and he welcomed you by name.

" '*How can Death be overcome?*' you said, and with eyes still closed he said, '*Make love to a woman.*' '*How can Death be overcome?*' you said as you lifted him from the sand, and he said, '*Do deeds worthy of poets.*' '*How can Death be overcome?*' you shouted a third time over the waves' roar, his face inches from yours as he opened eyes of a startling depth and clarity and said, '*There is a way.*'

"Following his advice, you left the Peloponnese and walked west over the mountains and past cities you'd never seen and in the lonely places when cruel-eyed men saw you from the woods they looked at each other and said, '*This one is mad, or holy, and in any case beyond the cares of men, so let him be.*'

"You walked a long way and it was only when you were resigned to walking forever that you came to the end, a cliff of black rock where the river Acheron cascades into a leaden sea. You built an altar out of broken stones for Hermes of the Boundaries and hunted animals and spilled their blood on the lichen-stained granite.

"Weeks went by, and then seasons, and every day was the same until the night you dreamed that a young man with golden hair stood beside the altar watching you sleep. '*You want too much,*' he said. '*But you're brave enough, and determined, and have the least self-ish of motives, so I'll give you a gift—you can see your friend once more.*' '*That's not enough,*' you said. '*Why should I help you?*' he asked coolly, and waited, and you could see he had all the time in the world, and then you screamed a scream that tore your throat and filled the night and you sustained it even as your breath faltered and your mind went dark. The youth's eyebrow lifted fractionally, and he said, '*Stay awake for seven days, and on the last night you'll see Death returning to his dolorous kingdom. He'll be weary, so seize him, if you can, and wrestle him down. Beat him and you can impose terms, though you'd be the first man ever to do it.*'

"You felt a giddy euphoria, though you knew your cause was desperate, for the great victory was finally at hand, and if you had to overcome a god to gain it, then so what, for you stood to gain everything, and had nothing to lose but the tag end of your mortal span. You sat on the cliff-edge, anticipating the struggle, grateful for the chance to prove yourself greater than every other man. By the third day the hours were a litany of agonies and it took all your hero's will and soldier's discipline to keep your eyes open, and by the fifth day you wanted to lie down on the black rock and close your eyes for just a moment, for just a moment couldn't matter, but you reminded yourself that seven days of suffering are as nothing beside eternity, and you reminded yourself of me. On the sixth day the skies glowed like lightning and voices whispered evil counsel in your ear and you thought you saw me sitting beside you, my arm around your shoulders, saying nothing, and you smiled at me and said I shouldn't worry, that you had it all in hand, that it wouldn't be long now, and then I was shouting at you, pleading with you to open your eyes as the black king striding by stooped to look at you sleeping with your chin on your hand; he shook his head and went on, though I cried out to him for mercy, not for me but for you as your dreams turned to boiling skies and burning oceans and weariness like a deep well down which you were falling, and when you woke you were alone and knew you'd slept a long time.

"You went back to Athens and never spoke of what had happened. They said you were a quieter man but a better king, and that something had gone out of you; you often passed the day sitting with your children in the sun, and later with your grandchildren, and the hero you'd been was indiscernible. Decades passed, and your strength waned, and then came the day when you saw the truth in your doctors' closed, politic faces.

"The next day you went to your great hall and summoned your family and your warriors and your courtiers and even your huntsmen and dogs. You told them it was time for a last great adventure, at which the drummers, who had been waiting, started playing, and in the din no one heard the men outside nailing the doors shut.

"When the drums stopped you said, *'Time burns away, as this palace burns away, and we will burn with it,'* and then they smelled the smoke. The men threw themselves at the doors, and hacked at them with their swords but all in vain. The burning air was unbreathable and the blackened floor buckling when someone choked, *'Why?'* You said, *'Doomed to die, I don't give up, and I have but a single enemy. As no other course is open, I'll bring war to shadow-lands, and shatter Death's kingdom with an army of ghosts.'* The hall's doors burst before a flood of black water that engulfed the men and their bronze swords and the dirty straw and the desperately paddling dogs and bore them away, and it was all you could do to keep hold of your sword as the churning water tumbled you through the dark until finally, gasping, you fought your way to the bank and dragged yourself up onto the shore of a river glittering blackly under a starry night.

"You dragged your liege-men from the river before they forgot themselves entirely, and soon the men and dogs huddled together, staring into nothing as though searching for words at the tips of their tongues. Only through kicks and blows could you rouse them to prise stones from the dry ground and build the listing approximation of a palace where you sat in state before your indifferent subjects and exhorted them to fight the final battle well, to do great deeds even here among the shadows, but their eyes were vacant and their sword-arms listless. Even you were reduced to the ceaseless recitation of your lineage and purpose, and you'd lost your first love's name, and your mother's face, and the names of all the dogs whose ghosts twitched restlessly at your feet, but not for one moment did you forget it was Death who was your enemy.

"Finally you took your spear and the handful of men lucid enough to follow and set off through the fields of asphodel and snow. You met shades who spoke of white cities, of sculpted valleys, of infernal palaces of bronze and basalt, but as you went on there was nothing but the dark plain before you and one by one your men slipped away, or forgot what they were doing, and it was always getting colder, and then you were trudging through the snow alone with nothing but your spear and your will burning like a blue sun to guide you.

"There wasn't much left by the time you saw a fire in the distance and heard me calling your name. I tried to be kind, but you wouldn't set aside your purpose, not for one moment, and so our youths are lost, and our lives, and now the last gift of the god."

I smile at him. "I have you at least, and that is much."

Pirithous's face, drained of everything. "Not even that," he says, and he and the fire vanish. Around me, the dark.

45

ASCLEPIOS

Theseus's wife Phaedra hanged herself over her af-
fair with her step-son Hippolytus. Hippolytus was
then put in the care of Asclepios, best among doc-
tors and Apollo's son. When Hippolytus died, As-
clepios brought him back to life with his father's help.

We rowed out at dawn, the slave, the boy and I. The
island was a shadow on the sea, then raucous wheeling gulls, sea caves and passages resonant with surf;
we waded through high water under low arches to
white sand beaches where the waves were a deep murmuring. Sea birds watched with ancient eyes as we
sprawled on rank grasses in the sun.

  Then the slave was carrying the child up the wet
sand, shouting. There was blood on the boy, whose
white skin had been as gold to me. The urchin's spines
were still embedded in his flesh—he wailed when I
touched them. He'd been swimming, had seen the sun
behind an urchin like a spiked aurora, aqueous light

radiating out around it in its hole, and he'd so wanted to touch the secret at its core. A surging wave had swept him in. Dreadful wounds, transpiercing him, and as his life coursed away he spoke of what he'd seen there, of the black plumes pouring out of him, the watchful dark things circling, their bodies patched with pale luminance.

I got all the spines out in time for him to know it. I laid them end to end in the sand, aligning their broken fragments just so.

And now the sun is going down, and though the island is behind us I know it's getting dark there, and that there will be no one to tend to him but the birds and the wind and the ancient things waiting in the reef, and that the waves will beat on the stone walls of the tunnel leading to the circular beach where his grave lies under the open sky. One day I'll go back and see if time has wound on there, or if with the loss of him the days stop.

He plays by a river of black water, setting stones in a pattern in the mud. The intensity of his absorption shows how alone he is.

I wake engulfed in loss. Moonlight glows through low clouds, and the wind comes from the sea. My mind is clear. I know what I'll do.

It's hard to work the boat alone, but it's a terrible thing I have planned, and I won't share the pollution.

On the island the tide has already come and gone

and scattered the low cairn I made. I dig through the wet, heavy sand and disinter his body. I clean him in the water. The last of his blood wells out and reddens a receding wave; I brush the scuttling crabs from his mouth and close his staring eyes.

One of my aunts—the kindest of them, and the wisest—once gave me a vial of what she said was Gorgon blood. I open the vial by touch, find the puncture wounds with my fingertips, and pour into each a single, careful drop. The wounds close like startled anemones, leaving only puckered scars. I put a hand on his cold chest, an ear to his blue mouth—nothing.

I call to him. Nothing but the waves. I call again, louder, and again, and still the clamor of the waves and wind, and I raise my voice over them, and over the tide, and over my own heart beating, and over all the roar of the world, again and again, and then I hear him, down by the water, singing quietly to himself. I walk down toward the break-line, and it's very dark, and the tide must have gone out because I walk a long way down the sand. I know I should have found the sea by now but I go on, for miles, it seems, and the sand is very dry, and then there's a river before me, cold, fast and black. The boy is on the bank, putting stones in a pattern in the mud.

He looks up when I touch his shoulder. I say, "It's time to go back."

"I'm not done yet," he says.

"You can finish later. There will be time."

Hand in hand we walk back up the beach but the

way is long, even longer than I remember, and it's getting steeper. Every step is an effort, and then an agony as the way rises and the sand yields under my steps, but the boy runs ahead and disappears. Soon I have to use my hands to climb up the crumbling dunes and then I'm about to fall (I know that to fall is to be lost forever) but then heat and light on me and my father is there, like the first red rays of dawn, laughing even in these shadows. He takes my hand and pulls me after him as he runs lightly over the sand which rises rapidly into a sheer wall and for a moment we're flying, and then, at last, I'm on the cold beach again, clutching the boy, who inhales spasmodically, his eyes roaming behind closed lids.

As I kiss his forehead a shadow falls. Death says, "You have robbed me, and you will pay."

46

ALCESTIS

After Asclepios offended Death, Death petitioned Zeus to kill him with his thunderbolts. Apollo retaliated by killing the Cyclopes who had forged them. Zeus then punished Apollo with seven years of servitude. Admetus, king of Pheres, bought Apollo in a slave-market, and was kind to him through the term of his bondage. Apollo then intervened with the Fates on Admetus' behalf, getting them to promise to let Admetus escape death when his time came if another would take his place.

Alcestis was Admetus' wife.

Someone is knocking on my door. I expect the maid but find it's my husband, who hasn't come to my room in years. At first I think he's drunk, and then I think he's ill, and then I think some god has possessed him because he bars the door, takes my face in his hands and says, "Death is right behind me, and to the shadow-lands I go."

As I look for words he says, "Death appeared like a black shadow on a burning world. *It's time,* he said, as I wrenched myself awake. I knew my arguments were futile even as I marshaled them but then through the fumes of sleep and my despair I remembered I had a way out. *Wait!* I said. *Not yet! Let me find another!* and fled as Death hesitated.

"I caromed through the freezing corridors, stumbling and panting, his measured footsteps close behind, and it seemed the palace was abandoned, that I would never find anyone at all, but then I saw my mother's door. Bursting in I said, *Death has come for me, unless another will take my place,* and I remembered how she'd loved me when I was a child, but she was very old and for a moment looked afraid, and then her face closed and with querulous petulance she said she was just an old woman and these phantasms had nothing to do with her. *He's right behind me,* I shouted, my voice raw, but she'd turned back to her loom and wouldn't raise her face again no matter how I pleaded and the footsteps were louder as I ran off again into the palace which seemed to have become a place I'd never known until I found the barracks where the captain of my guard sat oiling his javelins, and my heart rose to see him for he was a man of exacting discipline and proven loyalty—I'd lifted him up from poverty, and entrusted my life to him as a matter of course. I said, *My son, I need you, as I've never needed anyone,* and as he stood and drew his sword I saw in his eyes that he would fight to the death for me, and sick with

relief I explained what was happening and the footsteps echoed all around us and when I turned back to
him I saw he was weeping. He wouldn't meet my eyes
as he sheathed his sword and said, *I'm so sorry, sir—
forgive me*, but I was already running though my legs
were weak and I couldn't breathe the cold air and then
I burst into the hall where I found old friends and
men I'd made great and slaves I'd freed and soldiers
sworn in blood to me and old mistresses I'd treated
kindly after their beauty had gone; I went from each
to each, begging them to help me, but no one would
meet my eyes and no one even seemed to hear me and
our breath was white and the sun was lost in shadow
as Death came closer, his footsteps deafening, and I
fled into the corridor and I braced myself to make a
stand but my fingers were numb and when I drew my
sword it slipped from my hand to bounce and clatter
on the slick ice covering the floor, and then I fled a
last time and came here."

For a moment his fear infects me, but then I realize he's just old, and confused, and has had a bad
dream. I hush him, stroke his face and hair and tell him
not to worry. He doesn't resist when I put him in my
bed, where he hasn't been in a long time. "You stay
here and warm up. Everything's going to be fine," I
say with hearty conviction.

"But I must go," he says, "unless another will take
my place, and none will, for I'm friendless. Every oath
of love was empty, and now that the void is before me
every hand is snatched back, and so I fall."

"I'm sure someone will help you," I say, and think of calling for my maid, a doctor, anyone.

"In fact, I'm alone," he says, and, to my surprise, he kisses me, which he hasn't done in years, and I put my hand to my cheek, amazed, for in his watering eyes I see an openness and a clarity that I'd thought lost to our old detentes and clotted dislike, and behind the years his face is the face of the boy who once courted me. As he starts to rise he says, "My love, goodbye."

"No," I say. "You are not alone. I will go. *I* will take your place," and I mean it, though I have never been brave, and I fear death, and if I ever loved him it was long ago, but I can't bear to see his solitude.

Another knock at the door.

47

TIRESIAS

In life, Tiresias was a prophet. In death, he was the only shade who was fully awake.

Hades was bounded by Lethe, the river of forgetfulness.

I walk through the fog purposefully, as though I have a destination. There are others nearby, noiseless silhouettes in the translucent grey, but they're never close enough for me to see their faces. A flaw in the fog, and there before me is a warrior in bronze, blood leaking down his cuirass; I see his eyes through his helmet, and he seems to recognize me, but then the fog swallows him, and when I pursue him I find only footprints in dry sand.

There's the sound of rushing just before me, and I come to the bank of a wide river, its far side barely visible. When the others see it they run toward it and wade in, but I hesitate, looking down into the dark water, and then I see their faces as they rise streaming from the cold flow and how their joy has given way to blankness by the time they clamber up the far bank into fields of dust and cinder and asphodel protruding from torn earth, and at last I know where I am. I scramble back from the edge as eager shades push past me.

A youth with golden hair and a serpent twining around his staff sits on the bank beside me, chin on hand. He says, "The river brings peace, you know."

"No," I say convulsively. "I won't lose myself."

"Much is lost already. I don't think you even know your name."

"What's in a name?" I say, trembling. "Nameless, I'm still myself, not some empty shade sulking in the dark."

"The river is the salve to every woe. It's the end of every suffering."

I shake my head and clasp my arms to my chest, saying nothing.

"So be it," sighs the youth, standing. "You're unlikely to end up thanking me, but I'm used to being cursed for granting favors."

"Wait," I say, as he turns away. "Where will I go? What will become of me? Can I go back to the world?"

"Never," he says, "but all of Hell stands open."

I try to go back but a high wind buffets me and I find nothing but fog, sand and shades rushing by. I follow the river downstream, careful to stay dry, and eventually find stepping stones, barely protruding from the current, leading to the far side. Having nowhere else to go, I pick my way across, though the stones are slippery, and when I look into the flow I recognize dissolution. Strange to be here and have something left to lose.

The newly dead are confused when they clamber up the bank. They cry out to me, thinking I'm a god, or a lover, or their mothers, and I try to explain but they don't seem to hear me and soon blunder on into the fog.

The sky is a flat unchanging grey, and I can never see far. Having nothing to do, and all time before me, I decide I'll learn all of Hell's geography.

I find: empty cities, skewed and choked with dust, the buildings like worn teeth protruding from the sand, as though cities had souls and these were their wreckage. A field where stone doors lie scattered on the ground. A banquet hall abandoned but for two cadaverous men on granite thrones, one of whom stirs as I pass by. The endless dead, some walking steadily but most standing with their backs to the river, saying nothing, letting time flow by.

I hear the echo of music once, and my heart races but when I run toward the sound it fades out, never to return.

Sometimes I see Hermes in the grey fields. Often he'll postpone his business to talk with me, telling me the secrets of gods and of kings, though I know he's open with me only because there's nowhere I can go.

I find hills where the ancient dead wait, standing in ranks on the slopes' swell and fall. Heads bowed, eyes closed, all face the same direction. They seem to be waiting for something, though in this waste nothing happens.

I talk to them sometimes, and try to draw them out, but they rarely turn their dull eyes toward me. I ask questions; I touch their faces; I scream at them, my cries dissolving in the birdless silence. Now and then a ghost works its mouth around the dust of ages and its story comes tumbling out, though they seem not to know I'm listening. Theirs was an older Greece, the sun brighter, the sky more vivid, the islands in another order. Animals spoke, and gods and men lived together. They have no reserve, exposing old venality, cowardice, lawless pleasure, extravagant mortal rages. When their faces crumple I say don't worry, never mind it, everything's over for you. Their stories done, they fall silent, as though something's been used up in them, and gape listlessly, never to be roused again.

I go deep into the foothills, hoping to find some landmark, some break in the hills' undulations, but there are only silences and endless waiting ghosts, and this goes on and on, and one day I decide that, having come this far, I'll go on to the end.

Once the dead looked up as I passed but as the hills descend they're like stones lined up on the sand, worn by the wind, their features sculpted into polished masks. I press my hand to one and the stone under my palm dissolves into sand like the sand underfoot. As I go deeper the sand becomes finer, and soon the grains are fine as dust, as the sky is the color of dust, and there's never a wind here, and except for my footsteps the silence is total.

Time enough. There will be time enough. There will be time enough is what I say to myself, over and over, and these words are the rhythm that puts one foot before the other.

It's only when the hills have become a plain and the dead are eroded like stones in a river and I've nearly ceased to see the world that I realize I'm not alone, nor have been for some time. Death is beside me, and we walk together a long while and then I ask why these ghosts, why this dust, and where the plain is going.

There is a white city beyond the curve of the world, he says, *and what passes through its gates endures forever. This is Mnemosyne, the city of memory.*

"And is everything there?" I ask, my eyes tearing as I think of the years and loves that slipped away, but Death says, *Its gate is narrow, to keep out the world's profusion and redundancy, and the way is long, longer than ever you walked on earth, and most never come near it but wear away into rivers of sand, rubble of souls, fragments of memory. Nevertheless there are some few, mostly poets and mathematicians, who set off gladly, in the hopes that some part of them—a good phrase, or the intuition for a theorem—will pass through the gate and persist within the city.*

"Will they admit me?"

That city's judgments are unknowable.

He points the way down a path barely paler than the surrounding desert sand, and I'm alone now as I walk under neutral skies, and there are water stains on the dry slopes, and then they're gone, and I walk a long time, and I cease to see the sky, and I cease to see the path, and even the dead are gone, and there are only the odd stones scattered on the sand, and once a century a wind rises and moves them, and my hand before my face is the color of sand, and years slip by unnoticed, and the city is only an idea, and this desert's name is eternity, and the wind blows and fades and carries me along, and then, white towers.

PART VIII

APHRODITE, CONTINUED

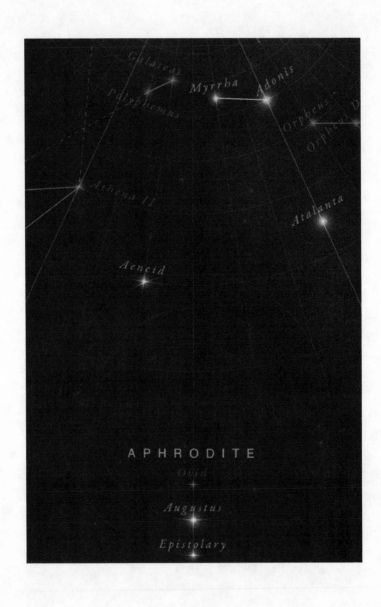

48

ATALANTA

Atalanta was beautiful, and a hero in her own right. She didn't want to marry. Aphrodite and Death conspired against her.

I was born with a beauty more than mortal and stood a head taller than the tallest of men. Every morning I went hunting in the hills, and I was always happy; I had friends then, the daughters of my father's courtiers, who rose with me at first light and tried to keep up. After the hunt we'd sprawl in the grass and watch the sky fade, and as the world lost its light it seemed every day would always be the same. They said my grandfather had been a god, and that it skipped generations, but I could never bring myself to care.

One day my friends and I were swimming in the river and I saw Hypermnestra smiling and staring into nothing as she wrung out her hair. She looked hunted when I asked what she was thinking, so I pressed her, and she admitted she'd taken a lover. I saw that she was lost, though we had all made promises, and for just a moment the future was colored by fear. "Get out of here," I said quietly, my contempt just contained; she clambered dripping up the bank, pulling on her chiton as we stood in the shallows, watching her leave.

She had her wedding in the Aphrodite temple in the woods. The old women wept and the little girls scattered flowers as I watched from the trees where the silence was such that I heard my pulse beating. There was an uncanniness in the stillness and a silent woman with shining golden hair watched me at a distance through the shadows of the branches but I recognized her face from the statues in the temple and ignored her as I did all wicked spirits and soon she disappeared. That night I thought of Hypermnestra and hoped even then she'd come back but the next morning I slept late and when I woke she'd already gone off to her new life of dullness and care, and as the week passed I heard nothing, and my mind drifted.

It wasn't long afterwards that my father asked me to walk with him. He said nothing on our first lap around his garden, and then, wringing his hands and looking away from me, he said it was time to think about a wedding.

"Whose?" I asked.

"Yours," he said.

My rage bloomed coldly and with deadly precision I said, "I will never marry."

"But you must," my father said, desperately reasonable, smiling foolishly.

In a flat, lethal voice I said, "I'll marry the first suitor who can out-run me, and be the death of all who can't."

He didn't mention it again, and I thought the crisis was past, and that everything would stay the same, but it wasn't long before another friend got engaged, and then another, and by the end of summer they were leaving me in a trickle and the next year they left me in a flood but by then I'd learned not to let it touch me. There were young girls just old enough for the hunt and I tried to talk to them but we hadn't grown up together and they were strangers who in any case seemed to be afraid of me, and soon I was hunting in the hills alone. For a while my rage came in gusts, and I was pitiless and killed wantonly, but it soon passed, and I forgot them.

I started spending most of my time in the hills, letting weeks go by without speaking, and sometimes felt I was becoming an animal. What I'd said to my father had faded from my mind but word must have gotten out because one day I found a young man waiting for me at a cross-roads. I saw the fear rising in his eyes as I came nearer—he'd believed in my beauty but not in my size—but he'd been raised to be brave and to strive relentlessly for victory. He said his name was Hippomenes, and his voice shook as he started in on his genealogy but I interrupted, saying, "Here are the terms: we race down this road to my father's gate. If you win, somehow, then that's one thing, but if you lose I'm going to put this arrow right through your heart," and I turned an arrow in my hand so that the razored bronze glinted in the sunlight; I'd only meant to scare him but saw that the threat had been a mistake—he'd been wavering, but I'd touched his pride and now he was going to race.

We ran down through the hills and for miles over the plain and then into the shadowed wood. He was an athlete, and we were side by side all the way. When my father's house appeared in the distance he put on a final burst, and he actually thought he was going to win, but in fact I'd kept pace with him only so he wouldn't give up, sneak off, and say he'd challenged me with impunity; even so, it rankled that he'd briefly thought himself my equal, and when we were twenty yards from the goal I blurred past him effortlessly and touched the gate-post. He'd been sprinting flat out and was still slowing as I turned to draw and string my bow in one motion. As I nocked an arrow a shadow fell on the world, though the sun was high in the cloudless sky; I'd killed many animals but never a man, but what, I thought, could be the difference, and I seemed to see him with greater vividness as he flung up his arms and shouted "No!" as I shot him in the heart.

He staggered backwards into the arms of a boy whose skin was white as marble, his blue veins glittering in the sun, and as he looked at me his stillness gave way to a longing and an avidity that made my skin crawl and no one had to tell me his name was Death. The blood reek was nauseating so I ran for it, Hippomenes' ghost close on my heels, squeaking and gesturing urgently like there was something he'd forgotten to tell me when he was alive, so I went all the faster, running for hours, sweat streaming, lost in motion, till I came to a fast river and dove into its green flow. I'd heard ghosts can't cross water so I stayed in the river till dusk and then I crawled shivering onto the far bank and fell asleep in the sand.

Years passed and my father became an old man but I didn't age so much as turn golden. I used every day, and loved velocity, but somehow the time seemed to go missing, the past was full of long swathes of nothing, as though familiar islands had disappeared into the sea. Now and then men came to try for me but most apologized when they saw me and stalked stiffly away; some pretended not to know who I was, acting as though they'd met me by chance while out walking. I often dreamed of the ghost of the boy who'd tried to be my lover, and I wanted to know what he'd wanted to say; whenever I saw him he was standing in the fields in the shadows of clouds and smiling at me but when I talked to him he'd only shake his head, and I'd wake with the feeling of loosing the arrow in my hand. Sometimes I saw the woman with the shining hair watching me from the wood, and when I did I stopped and waited, daring her, for I knew I was the direst thing in those hills, but she'd always just smile at me, as though she knew something I didn't, and then vanish.

I saw Melanion in the distance at the cross-roads on the hottest day of the year. I could have gone around him but saw no need to cede the road and didn't want it said I'd retreated. Up close I saw that he was a tall man, and beautiful the way that horses are; he didn't flinch when he saw me and a shadow settled on my heart as he looked into my eyes and said calmly that he knew the terms and wanted to race.

We started running and it was less like a race than like keeping him company. He was one of the fastest men I'd seen, though no match for me, and when we finally came under the cover of the wood I shot ahead, leaving him to plod on alone. Half a mile later he rounded a bend and found me waiting in the middle of the road. "Go home," I said. "No one saw you come, and no one will see you go. Tell people you couldn't find me, or that you changed your mind, but in any case go." I was offering him his life but instead of leaving with it he stepped forward and said, "No one will see . . ." The golden-haired woman was holding her breath as she watched from the trees and he was so close I could smell his sweat and then his fingertip brushed my clavicle. For the space of a breath I did nothing, and then my knife flashed through the air toward his cheek. He staggered back, sobbing, half his face slathered red; "*Run for your life*," I said, and he did.

It wasn't long until the day I woke early to shadows that seemed sharper and a new watchfulness in the hills. I was angry as I went out into the cold air with my arrows clattering in my quiver, for I knew, as animals know, that I was being hunted, and I wasn't surprised when I saw someone waiting at the cross-roads. He was little more than a boy, standing there, and as pale as the moon, blue veins glittering in the long early light. As I steamed in the cold I felt his chill.

He said, "*Race with me to your father's gate.*"

"What are the stakes?" I asked.

"*If I win, you come to my kingdom.*"

"And if you lose?"

"*Then every morning will be the first day of summer, and your friends will come back and never leave again, and everything will always stay the same.*"

Despite the glittering menace behind his words I couldn't keep from grinning, and my heart was light as I said, "*Go.*"

He was as fast as the west wind, and I loved him for it, and I ran flat out from the start. My shadow flying over broken stones in the waste by the road and the air was my medium as I pushed off from the dust for to run is to fall and I fell without end as the road had no end and in that morning I was outside of time, and untouchable, and I left him behind.

I streaked on for miles, alone and lost in motion as I shot over the plain and into the wood and there was only the sweet sting of my breath and the chaos of passing branches. It had been a long time since I'd seen him and I heard no panting, no pounding feet, no sound in the wood but birds singing and the wind, and my skin felt electrified. I finally slowed on a rise and looked back—I could see miles of road behind me but there was nothing there, not even a plume of dust.

I started walking toward my father's house, some-
what nonplussed to have beaten the great adversary so
easily. This is victory, I thought; the sky was beautiful, the first in an infinite succession of beautiful skies,
and I smiled because I'd won everything and I knew
I was capable of anything at all and then I noticed
that the woman with the shining golden hair was
keeping pace with me in the wood. "What do *you*
want?" I called in high good humor, and I wondered
how long she'd been following me, and then I saw that
she was beckoning. I looked back down the road—
still empty—and when I looked back she was disappearing into trees. "Wait," I said, pushing into the
foliage, my heart beating wildly, and I thought she'd
gone but then I saw a flash of white among the leaves,
and I pursued as she retreated, the branches whipping
my face. I found her chiton pooled on the bare earth,
and then I burst into a clearing where the light daz-
zled me, and there she was, right before me, close
enough to touch. The world fell away as my eyes followed the lunar surface of her skin to the sun burning
on the golden apple in the delta of her thighs.

When I rose from the grass she was gone. I'd closed my
eyes for a little while but it didn't seem like it could
have been very long, and I could still see the depres-
sion in the grass where she'd lain. Then I remembered
I was racing for my life, which might be forfeit already.
I threw on my tunic and tore through the trees to the

road and though the sun was lower in the sky there was still no sign of him but for all I knew he'd long since come and gone. It occurred to me to run away and not come back but it wasn't in me to flee and I told myself to make the best of my disadvantages and ran flat out for home. When I finally saw the gate-post he wasn't there, in fact no one was there at all; it was just another day, the cattle lowing in their paddock, and somewhere children shouting. I nocked an arrow and waited for him all that day, determined to wreck him, but he didn't come that evening or the next or in any of the long days of the summer which was the sweetest I'd known, as sweet as the wine I started drinking, as sweet as the mouths of the girls and the boys. I was more often in company, and ran less, and it wasn't long before I noticed that my wind wasn't what it had been, and I wondered if somewhere I'd made a mistake, but soon I was distracted because against all expectation I married, for love, I thought, but love faded, but it didn't matter because by then I had a daughter to whom I gave everything, and she looked much like me, if not quite so tall, but soon enough she ceased to need me, and once I heard her tell her friends that her mother had been an athlete once, though now it was hard to see. She married and went away, and then my husband died, and I spent my days working in my garden and walking in the hills where I'd once run, until the day I came home and found Death waiting at the gate-post.

49

MYRRHA

Myrrha crept into her father's bed one night, inspired by Aphrodite. Myrrha's son by her father was Adonis.

Aphrodite says, "Padding footsteps' soft approach and the hiss of her body sliding in beside you. The cold air, her heat beneath you, and her skin tastes like lemons and summer. Still asleep, you see the white moonlight on her wide, stricken eyes which tear as she looks up at you. You feel as though you've been reprieved, that time has restored what it took away— you thought you'd never see your wife again, but here she is, young again, though she's been dead twenty years, lost giving birth to your daughter. Inference stirs sluggishly but doesn't quite surface, and you remember that a city is like a circle of light where laws govern the lives of men, and even now you are leaving that illumination and going out into the night, and you know you must stop, but then I'm there and my breath is like fire as I whisper, *All laws are lies but mine*, and as the girl's thigh spasms you go sifting down into the dark. Soon it will be day and you will wake alone, wash carefully, and there might never have been a night."

50

ADONIS

Adonis was the lover of both Aphrodite, the goddess of love, and Persephone, the goddess of death. He got Aphrodite pregnant. He ended up dividing his time between them.

Light filters through the oaks as cicadas drone the day away and my lassitude is such I think I'll never move again. But then, in the hottest part of the day, she's there with me, all golden hair and hunger, and the sweat and heat are all but intolerable. Finally I wade in the frigid brook and when I turn back she's gone and night's coming.

Under the moon the world turns to bone and with spear in hand I course tirelessly over the undulating hills. A clattering in the bracken, then a deer's silhouette on a ridge; I give chase and soon bring it down. The deer's fat crackles over the fire and my shadow looms long on the trees; every nocturnal thing must see me, but there's nothing I fear in the night.

Then I see her, the pale one, very still as she watches me through the low branches. She strokes my hair and kisses my scratches with cold lips, puts my arrowheads in her mouth and coats them with black venom. She tries to draw me away with her but I tell her I love another; she says this is a mere passing affair, and will end soon. When she goes the sun is rising.

One morning I drowse with my head on my golden lover's smooth thighs, her fingers tangled in my hair, and I see her stomach is distended. I touch her but there's none of the heat and tautness of infection. What does this mean, I ask, and she says it means things are changing. No change, I say. Let everything remain exactly as it is. It can't, she says. It must, I say. There's always a way.

That night I go to the chalk valleys (the pale woman's yellow eyes follow me from the trees) and flush a black boar with tusks like dirty white sickles. Reeds breaking, creek's churn, and my arrows piercing only earth as he flies into a copse atop a hill. I rush in with spear raised but the trees end and beyond them there's a wide plain, white under the moon. A long road like a silver river cuts across the plain and leads to a faint shimmering in the farthest distance. The pale woman is beside me then, her fingertips brushing my arm. She says it's her city at the end of that road, and she'll wait for me there.

The dawn is sticky and hot and I wait by the brook but my golden lover doesn't come, not even when the sun is high in the sky. I look for her but find only bird-song and deer-trails and the cicadas' drone. Without her the forest is a waste and I'm restless, sitting in the shade, pitching stones in a brook, and finally I go to the hill and watch the road. In the distance I see a plume of dust and I know I'll soon be going.

51

AENEID

Aeneas was a prince of Troy and the son of Aphrodite. When Troy fell he fled to Italy and founded Rome.

Many centuries later the Roman poet Virgil recounted Aeneas' exploits in his Aeneid. *The emperor Augustus was Virgil's patron.*

His mother's bloom was as the springtime, but Aeneas had gotten old. He was a good suzerain to the kingdom he'd carved out of Italy, but privately he was detached, aware that any one of his carls could play the part as well, and that everything that made him Aeneas—the duel with Diomedes, the flight from Troy's ashes with his father on his back, sending Turnus sprawling to spill his lifeblood on the white Latin dust—was in the past.

His mother was watching when he hung his sword on the wall for good, and when he gave his favorite horse to his grandson; the gelding, feeling her presence, rolled his eyes and whickered at the mares. She watched him sleep some nights, pitying his old man's wheeze and rattle. Mortal mothers, she reflected, miss the season of their sons' decline.

One day as he walked through the dusty oaks around his fields a weight seemed to strike him in the chest and he fell to his knees among the acorns. The speckling of sun through the leaves overhead faded to spattered light in darkness and as at a distance he saw the cowherd who found him, the fingers probing his neck, the hand checking for breath and then closing his eyes, his wife wailing in the forest, the contained grief of his sons, the eldest of whom held a torch to a pyre of dry sticks and just as the world turned to flame his mother swept him into her arms and away.

There were white clouds and blue sky and wind with a hint of the sea. She carried him as easily as if he'd been a child, his cheek sinking into her breast, and he was ashamed at how much he was comforted. Should pride, he wondered, survive death? "Zeus loves me well," she said, kissing him. "For you, my only son, I begged the boon of immortality—once is enough, I said, to pass through the bitter gates of Hell.* Zeus said, *Seize him before his soul takes flight and take him to the marches of the underworld. There submerge him in the Styx, which will wash away every mortal part of him—what is left will live forever.*"

---

*As a young man Aeneas ventured into Hell and met the shades of his ancestors and descendants.

Aeneas opened his mouth to speak but wind ripped the words away as they hurtled down through shining gulfs of air and nothingness into dark canyons full of bats and sulfur and the smell of old stone and finally to low banks of black sand beside the glass-smooth Styx.

Its water swirled around her flushed calves as she pushed him under the swift flow which churned and ran red, and she cried out as his body dissolved like wet paper. Her wicked mind filled with blood and she thought of the wretched, humiliating passions to which even the strongest of the gods could be subjected. Then she saw the written sheets drifting away from where her son had been; she gathered up as many as she could but some were carried off by the current and others reached the black beach where a shade, or not a shade but a dreaming sleeper's ghost stooped, picked one from the flow, and looked at her with lucid eyes. At last, she understood. She said, "All for you, my Virgil."

52

AUGUSTUS

Gaius Octavius Augustus was the first emperor of Rome. He was prone to sleeplessness and bad dreams. He exiled Ovid.

Snow swirls over the fires of the legion in the high mountain pass. There's no sound but the wind's moan, the tents' rattle; the legionnaires' eyes follow Augustus as he walks past them toward the peak.

Cresting the pass, the plain opens up below him, ablaze with the flickering campfires of the Gauls, their army so vast its innumerable fires seem to reach the horizon where they commingle with the stars. The nearest barbarians are so close he can see their seamed and bearded faces, which show not rancor but resignation— they stare up at him as though to say, *With so many pushing behind us, what can we do but go on?*

He tries in vain to count their multitudes, hoping his trembling will be attributed to the cold. He imagines Rome sacked and smoldering, for Rome, however great, is but a single city, while the northern forests are illimitable, and how can so many be overcome?

The fire-light glitters on the glass jewels and crude weapons of the Gauls, who are brave men but simple, and he remembers that even their chieftains are afraid of storms, eclipses, witchcraft and ghosts, greedy for minted gold and the voluptuousness of cities, that they make war on Rome out of envy as much as ambition, and then he has it: instead of slaughtering them, or trying to, he'll found new Romes, other Romes on the far side of the Alps to absorb the tribes and make them citizens, and each wave of invaders will become a bulwark against the next, and instead of slowly crumbling the Roman frontier will move north over the black and dripping forests, the jagged mountains, the boundless tundra, and then over seas and down centuries to remote islands, distant continents . . .

But if Rome goes from a single city to a constellation of cities where Latin is a temple language and the eagle standard is taken for the votive of some raptor-hearted god then has he secured Rome's glory or just its dissolution, and how will he be remembered, and will his life and empire have meant nothing?

Now he's down on the plain in what had been the far distance. The barbarians are restive shadows and looking up he realizes that what he'd taken for stars are something else, are in fact the shining ranks of the glorious dead. They loom over him, radiant and still. Will he one day be among them? Now one burns so brightly he thinks it's the rising sun, but no, its light is cold—it's Alexander.

53

EPISTOLARY

Ovid was a Roman poet. Augustus exiled him to the Black Sea. Ovid never saw Rome again.

Ovid is finishing a letter. The wind from the plain slips through the cracks in the walls and the pen trembles in his hand as he writes out the last words and his thoughts turn toward home. He seals it and addresses it to the emperor of Rome—once an intimate, now almost a fiction of his memory—and hands it to the courier waiting by the door. Ovid stands in the street, watching the grey plume of the courier's dust rise up, dissolve.

The courier rides swiftly across the plain, his face set, his strength such that it seems he must soon reach his destination, but in fact everything is against him— the broken roads, the sun like a hammer, the night sky rent by thunderstorms that saturate the dust and send floods foaming through the washes and arroyos. He fords trunk-entangled rivers, wakes shivering in dripping, wind-tormented woods, comes to rain-swept cross-roads where loitering renegades oil knives beneath black gallows.

The letter suffers on the road, soaked in rain, stained with silt, slashed by the thief he left face-down in milky ditch-water. By the time he finds the squat tower of unmortared stones where the next courier waits, his face is gaunt, his quiver empty, the soiled letter coming apart.

The new courier's road winds up through a dry, dreary country of starry nights and empty desert space. Miles from anything, he notices that the letter's seal has rotted and fallen off. His conscience flares, flickers, dies; opening it, he finds the letter water-stained and mildewed, some lines blurred irretrievably, but still he can discern a story of exile and despair, of a message transformed in its passage through many hands on its way to a reader who is most likely a mirage.

He has the letter by heart, or nearly, when he finds the next courier by a dry well in an oasis. (In dreams he sees it written in letters of light on pages of wavering flame.) Only when his successor can recite the letter verbatim does he give him the rotting, sporadically legible scrap of paper and send him off.

Weeks pass before the new courier rides into a town and once the key for the Inn of the Couriers has been found and the inn opened (the townsmen had come to think of it as a crypt, or the temple of some dead religion) he finds pen and paper among the dusty rooms and transcribes what he remembers though he fears the falsity of memory and that the words have been shifted, transposed, rearranged. The original has disintegrated by the time he finds the next courier who takes the new letter and heads toward the mountains and away.

It isn't long before the letter has passed out of Latin and into the native tongues of the couriers or of the peoples they ride past—the men who worship fire, the ones who wear peaked caps and live in excavated mountains, the ones who dwell in houses built by riverbanks on stilts. Some regard this as an outrage, though others claim that the letter was never in Latin at all, that Ovid had in fact adopted the barbarous tongue of the Getae or the harsh lingua franca of the mercantile Greeks. Some couriers, carrying the letter only in their memories, find they have no tongue in common with their successors, and for a moment the letter passes out of language altogether and into gestures—they pretend to weep, to wrestle with brigands, to fend off the short, sharp arrows of the Scythians—or even objects—arrows laid in parallel in the dust, a broken plume, stones piled up in the semblance of a city.

Countless letters are in circulation now, and some trace their ancestry to the original, but all, by now, are corrupt, little more than florilegia of ghost stories, quotations out of context, fragments of geography. Through the incessant operation of chance some few have come to resemble their original, but there's no way to find them.

The false and worthless letters are as numerous as

the grains of sand in a desert but not even one has come within a hundred miles of Rome, or even a thousand, or even to a city where they fear the eagle-standard, where Rome is more than a rumor. In fact, it's generally agreed that Rome has long since fallen, that the city on the Tiber is no more than a ruin where goats browse on thistle among toppled colonnades. Some insist that Rome never existed at all, that there was only ever the idea of an empire, of a city as desirable as it is remote, ruled over by an emperor sitting in his summer palace, chin in hand, gazing out into the evening as the settling dimness swallows the city, the roads, the arbors, and at his elbow sits a letter unnoticed. If ever he were to open it (but his mind is elsewhere, and he almost certainly won't) he would read of a poet who was once almost an intimate, finishing a letter with shaking hand as, without hope, his thoughts turn toward home.

NOTES

NOCTURNE
Elpenor fell from the roof of Circe's house on Aiaia and broke his neck. His ghost wandered restlessly until he was buried.

ARACHNE
Ovid thought the gods were absurd—at one point he has Athena pole-vault out of a scene on her spear. I, too, am unlikely to invoke Athena Nike in time of crisis, but I'm interested in the gods as primes and essences, and have more regard for the dignity of these faded but august imaginary beings.

NEMESIS
Witches' duels are problematic—if both combatants can take any shape they like, the fight seems necessarily inconclusive—how does one do harm in such a battle, and why does Zeus, for all his power, act like a boorish mortal prince?

ATHENA I
If the world is Zeus' dream, the things he can't forget will tend to persist.

Traditionally, Athena sprang fully armed and armored from Zeus' skull after he swallowed the titan Mnemosyne.

IDEOGRAPH
I've always wanted there to be myths about language—what could be more fundamental?

ICARUS
In the original, Icarus melted the wax that held his wings together by flying too close to the sun. In Ovid's day no one had been higher than a mountaintop, or knew it was a journey of about ninety-three million cold, vacuous miles to the sun. My Icarus keeps trying to break out of the atmosphere, like a bird dashing itself against a window—he gets as far as its boundary, which is, I admit, not possible with no oxygen and a pair of home-made wings.

MINOS
The math in this story is abstract and magical. In essence it's a locked-room mystery about friendship and identity.

In the original, Minos tracked down Daedalus by offering a reward to anyone who could thread a string through a nautilus shell. Daedalus did it by tying a string to an ant and sending the ant through the shell. Minos went to the city where Daedalus was staying but was killed in his bath.

DAEDALUS
An irrational number is an infinite abyss, though they're present even in simple geometric objects like circles and squares. The ancient Greeks knew this, and were horrified.

PHILEMON AND BAUCIS
In the original, Philemon and Baucis were turned into trees immediately, which seems like a poor reward.

NARCISSUS
Ovid changed the Narcissus story—before him, Narcissus and Echo were unconnected. In his version there's a little etiology, and a nice image of vanity, but the interest of the story seems somehow occluded. I think of this story as a sort of complex organic molecule—the laws of physics are always trying to find a more compact configuration at a lower energy state—in my version Narcissus is warned of mirrors, but the mirror is Echo.

MEDEA II
This story is an indirect descendant of Kafka's "The Truth about Sancho Panza," and perhaps Wilde's "The Fisherman and His Soul."

JASON
A man comes home to find his dead father sitting on his doorstep, a young man again but instantly recognizable. Perhaps this is an image from an ancient tradition.

THETIS
In the original, Peleus catches Thetis with a net, though subduing a shape-changer seems very difficult, not to say a lost cause.

HELEN
The Greeks wanted to believe that the Homeric heroes were virtuous. It was therefore inadmissable that Helen gaily went off with Paris to Troy—it was suggested a phantom went in her place, an

idea I take up, but without any commitment to her probity. In some accounts Helen was the daughter of Nemesis and Zeus.

ELYSIUM

Negative after-lives are easy to imagine, but happy ones are harder to pin down. Here, Menelaus' paradise is an unbounded collecting expedition, which might have appealed to Charles Darwin, at least as a young man, or Stephen Maturin.

MIDAS

In the original there's an ironic twist and a moral lesson to be careful what you wish for and some nicely horrific imagery when Midas accidentally turns his wife into a gold statue. I changed it so that it's about the death of passion with middle age and an etiological story about the invention of money, which seems like a necessary myth for our time and perhaps all future ones.

PENTHEUS

In the original, Dionysos' maenads, Pentheus' mother among them, tore Pentheus apart.

Dionysos is a god of transformation. In *The Bacchae*, Pentheus is perhaps not entirely mature, but what if he had been disciplined and dutiful, not the kind of man to have his head turned by a drunken orgy—how would Dionysos get to him?

DAPHNE

In the original, Daphne was turned into a laurel tree to save her from Apollo's advances. In this version, Apollo has his way with her at no greater cost than understanding her vanity.

ACTAEON

In the original, Artemis sweeps water at Actaeon, turning him into a stag who is then killed by his own dogs. Ovid gives a full catalog of the many dogs' names, which is interesting mostly in that dogs got the same kinds of names then as they do now. One of the functions of art is to fill time—this was part of poetry's job in the early days of imperial Rome, but now people are more likely to binge-watch shows on-line.

PERSEPHONE

I once heard a friend tell her daughter, "One day you'll hear my voice coming out of your mouth and then I'll have won."

This story is perhaps more about Inanna than Persephone and Demeter.

THESEUS

Gilgamesh is present in this story.

TIRESIAS

Tiresias lived for seven mortal spans, and was the only fully lucid shade in the underworld.

ATALANTA

In the original, Atalanta is the equal of the best warriors of her time. She's running a footrace with a suitor when, despite a lifetime of war-like seriousness, she's distracted by an apple made of gold, loses the race and must therefore marry. To lose everything for a bauble seems inconsistent with her character.

I envisioned Atalanta as about six foot five, very butch and more inclined toward the divine side of her nature, which means she's more or less abstained from the mess of mortal life, until she makes a little mistake, and lets Death in, and he and Aphrodite conspire to undo her. Even then, she'd have prevailed, had she not been distracted by Aphrodite's mons veneris—what else could the golden apple be?

AUGUSTUS

One explanation for Rome's success is that instead of enslaving or robbing the people of conquered cities, it made them Roman citizens.

Like most conquerors, Augustus compared himself to Alexander the Great.

His reason for exiling Ovid is unclear—Ovid said it was for "a mistake and a song."

ACKNOWLEDGMENTS

Thanks to Bronwen Abbattista, Bill Clegg, Cordelia Derhammer-Hill, Vasiliki Dimoula, Jonathan Galassi, Linley Hall, Cole Harkness, John Knight, Simon Levy, Isidora Milin, Phong Nguyen, Elena O'Curry, Nalini Rao, Shawna Yang Ryan, the Santa Maddalena Foundation, Emmeline Sun, Spring Warren and Rebecca Vaux.

Thanks also to Publius Ovidius Naso. Homer seems like a figure out of the dream-time, but Ovid is recognizably a man. I'm grateful for his poetry and regret his trouble.